Stories I Like to Tell

– Book 4 –

Pam —

A YEAR OF

WONDER

A year of stories.

Enjoy!

JERRY PETERSON

JOHN SMITH

WINDSTAR PRESS

DEDICATION

To Marge Smith Peterson, Jerry's wife and first reader. Marge also is John's grandmother.

To Jay and Ruthann Smith, John's parents.

To the members of Jerry's writers groups, *Tuesdays with Story* and *Stateline Night Writers*.

And to a friend and one-time colleague who prefers to remain unnamed.

ACKNOWLEDGMENTS

From Jerry . . . This is the sixteenth book I've published as indie author, this one under my Windstar Press imprint.

We indies do call on others to help us make our books the best that they can be. I can't design a cover. I don't have the eye or the technical know-how to create a cover that is certain to stop a potential reader, grab her or him and say this is a book you've absolutely have to buy. Dawn Charles of Book Graphics has that eye and the technical know-how. She's a superb cover designer. This cover is hers as are most of the others that front my books.

Just as a knock-out cover is vital to grabbing potential readers, so are the words on the back cover, words we call the blurb . . . words from another writer who has read the book and knows how good it is. For those words, this time I turned to fellow short story writer Ted Hertel. His stories appear in a number of anthologies, most recently in *To Hell in a Fast Car.*

I always close with a thank you to all librarians around the country. They, like you and your fellow readers who have enjoyed my James Early mysteries, my AJ Garrison crime novels, my John Wads crime novellas, my Wings Over the Mountains novels, and my short story collections, have been real boosters. Without them and you, there would be no reason to write.

A NOTE FROM JERRY

This book is special, a joint project with my grandson, John Smith . . . the REAL John Smith as he will tell you when you and he meet. Incidentally, I use John's line–the REAL John Smith–in my December story, "One Alone."

While I'm a novelist, I've been writing short stories for a long time, more than a quarter century. John discovered he had a gift for writing short stories only a few years ago, when he took a creative writing class as a student at KM Perform, the Arts & Performance Academy at Kettle Moraine High School in Wales . . . that's Wales, Wisconsin.

I began to vibrate. So last year, when John enrolled at the University of Iowa and signed up for a creative writing course there, I asked him whether he'd like to collaborate on an anthology of short stories.

I outlined the concept for a book . . . we each write a story a month for a year. Twenty-four stories total.

John said yes.

And this book is the result.

As you read along, you will discover that John's specialty is flash fiction . . . tightly written, super short stories, often less than a thousand words.

In contrast, I tend to write long. Three of my stories in this collection—"Digging in the Dirt," "The Forever Deputy," and "One Alone"—each run more than 6,000 words.

So there you have our story.

Now enjoy The J&J Anthology or, as we have titled it, *A Year of Wonder.*

January

Three really short stories about January
by John

I LOOK OUT and see the streets are full of trash. Happy New Year, Manhattan.

POLLY LAID in her casket. "This is comfy," she said.

MY BROTHER came home in January wearing a uniform. "Ma, Pa. I've grown up."

Spring Fantasies
by Jerry

THE WEATHER OUTSIDE is not frightful, but the wind is piling up three-foot drifts in the backyard.

Do I care?

Not really.

You see, I'm inside, comfortably reclined in my Barcalounger, a mug of hot chocolate on the table by my elbow, and I'm sorting through the latest dream books that have come in the morning mail:

Gurney's

Field's

Park

Eden Brothers

Seed Saver Exchange

High Mower Organic

The Cottage Gardener

Burpee

Ah, Burpee, the good old standard.

Mister Burpee—W.A.—started his business a hundred forty years ago, when he was a 14-year-old kid. He sold baby chicks by mail, only to discover that his customers really wanted seeds for the garden and the fields. So that's the direction he went, and, by 1915, he was mailing more than one million catalogues to gardeners around the country each year during the depths of winter.

The post office loved him.

One thing that set Mister Burpee apart from his competitors was his plant breeding program. Out of it came a wealth of new varieties including, yes, Iceberg lettuce, Golden Bantam sweet corn, the burpless cucumber, and the Big Boy tomato . . . the first of the really large tomatoes any gardener could grow.

And here it is on page 3, Burpee's newest, the Burpee Steakhouse Hybrid, produces tomatoes so large that it takes a small child to pick one up. There's a picture here to prove it. Got to put that on the order sheet.

Anyone can grow patio tomatoes, but here on page 25 are a host of vegetables Burpee developed for the home gardener who doesn't have any garden space, who intends to grow his or her vegetables in a pot . . . King Harry, Red Cloud, Yukon Gold, and Russian Banana potatoes; a variety of beets, a host of specialty lettuces, Yaya hybrid carrots, and salt wort, whatever that is. A note says salt wort is great in salads and with sushi. And Burpee also has for the container gardener radishes, cucumbers, summer squash, eggplant, sweet yellow peppers, and–get this–sweet corn . . . On Deck Hybrid Supersweet Sweet Corn, the first variety ever developed, the catalogue says, that can be grown in a bucket of dirt. Gotta try that. Only $6.95 for a packet of seeds.

When I lived in Kentucky, I fought my way through blackberry and raspberry patches, coming out with pails full of berries at the price of torn shirt sleeves and arms scratched bloody.

Thorns, those dang-blasted thorns.

One year, my mother-in-law had had enough. She planted thornless blackberry canes. Prolific with berries bigger than the first joint of your thumb . . . and no scratches.

Made me a believer.

Burpee has its own thornless variety, the Triple Crown Blackberry. Says here on page 44 that it produces fruit over a five-week season. That's good.

Five bare-root plants for $32.95.

Well, I can buy a lot of Lanacane and band aids for that. But the pain I'd still have to deal with . . .

The Triple Crowns go on the order form.

Summer wouldn't be summer without watermelons. For a period of time, I lived and worked in Kansas and got to know one of the men who worked with the plant breeders at Kansas State University who developed the Crimson Sweet. Went to field days where the melon was served. Oh, that was so good.

Let's see what Burpee has . . . There it is on page 37, yes, the Crimson Sweet. The fruit, though, comes in at around 25 pounds, good if you're having a party, but not for two people. Oh, here it is on page 40. No, that's not it. That's a Carolina Cross, an heirloom melon that produces fruit weighing 200 pounds. We'd have to have a block party if we grew one of those.

Turn back a page.

This is it.

This is the one I want, the Big Tasty Hybrid. The fruit, it says, is 12 inches around and weighs between six and eight pounds. And no seeds to spit out.

Excellent.

A packet of 10 seeds for $5.95. Ten seeds will produce enough melons for the neighborhood.

Dare I try a pumpkin? My luck in the past as a pumpkin grower was not good. I've gone to several state fairs where the champion pumpkins have weighed in at upwards of three-quarters of a ton and more. By the way, the world record is 2,323.7 pounds, that pumpkin grown in Germany two years ago by a Mister Beni Meier.

Bidding for seeds from which to grow giant pumpkins—yes, seeds for the best are sold exclusively at auction—frequently starts at $15 for one seed and goes up in $5 increments. So you could pay $30 to $40 for one seed, more sometimes if you want a seed from a record holder.

A packet of seeds on page 47 in the Burpee catalogue for Connecticut Field Pumpkins, a standard that commercial growers love, sells for $3.95.

You know what I'm thinking?

I'm thinking I'll wait until fall and buy my jack-o-lantern pumpkin at the grocery store for, oh say, $3.95.

February

The Purple Paper Eater
by John

"If you ever had the wonderment of wondering
why bureaucratic paperwork takes forever,
here is the secret."

IT WAS DEFINITELY the end of February in Minnesota. The slush and snow melted together to form a puddy that was simultaneously wet and sticky. The rocks and pebbles in the softening ice gave it a grainy look. It was cloudy and cold, yet humid enough to make me uncomfortable. And to make matters worse, I had to go to the DMV.

Ding! The bell over the door sounded, letting everyone know I was there. I heard grunts from the civil servants at the counters. The only happy face in the room was that of a woman on a poster that said, "Driving safely is the key to a happy life." She obviously had never had to go to the DMV…

"What are you here for?" a woman with a grumbly voice asked.

"Renewing my license," I said.

She wore a perfume that smelled like it belonged to her great grandmother and her red lipstick outlined years of passive aggression, sarcasm and self-loathing.

She glared at me. "Fill these papers out, your number is forty-four. Next, please."

I smiled at the woman, but she was through with me.

The papers I filled out were . . . boring. There is no need to talk about them. I filled in my name, my social security number, etc. There were a lot of forms. I filled in my name, social security number, etc. Another form: name, social security, etc. Another form: namesocialsecurityetcnamesocialsecurityetc.

Everything blended together, and after twenty minutes of mindless, hypnotic bureaucracy, someone called my number.

"Forty-four," a sibilant voice announced over the loudspeaker. "Forty-four."

The voice was meek with a nervous shake in it.

I headed to the farthest counter on the left. The light there flickered, and the chair's cushioned seat across the counter was torn, as if a slasher had run by wielding a machete. The walls to either side of the booth were cracked and their one-time shade of off-white had aged to an eerie yellow. The second I came into his area, it felt like I was in a different world, like the DMV had disappeared.

I stepped up to the counter to find a hunchbacked man in a purple polo shirt that seemed to be three sizes too small. He was muttering

9

something to himself.

"Hello," I said.

He dropped his papers, as if I had startled him.

"Oh, I'm so sorry," I said, and I meant it.

"It's alright. Just some papers, nothing too special." Yet, the man went sputtering around his area, picking up the papers that had gotten away. I noticed the answers called for in every blank of every page were written in purple ink. I had always thought black was the official color for this.

He grunted something that sounded like relief as he gathered up the final piece, like the paper was something dear to him, something lost that now had magically been found. He kissed the page as he came back to the counter.

His face, I noticed one lens in his glasses was cracked, maybe even a chip out of it, and he had a wart to the right of his eye. His nose was bent, like it had been broken in a fight. And his eyes, he didn't look at me, but everywhere else.

His cubicle, it was surreal. The light continued to flicker, and the computer on the counter, to me it was a dust collector it was so old.

"What can I help you with?" he asked, breathing hard from the effort of corralling all those papers.

"I just need a renewed license."

"Ah, just one moment, please." He pulled open the drawer of a filing cabinet—the drawer next to the bottom—and shuffled through each folder until he found the one he was looking for.

He slammed the drawer closed and slapped the folder on the counter. "Here we are. License renewal forms."

He licked his fingers and slid them across the top of the folder, opening it.

A line of blood spewed across the folder, but the man seemed not to notice.

"Here we go . . . oh! Would you look at that, a cut," he said and popped his fingers in his mouth. He held them there for an uncomfortably long time.

At last he sighed and dealt me the top page from the folder.

"Fill this out," he said, never making eye contact. "And, ah, please use this."

He handed me a purple pen.

With reluctance, I took the pen and wiped the blood away with a tissue.

The form again called for the standard stuff: name, social security number, etc. He stared at me while I was filled it out, his breathing intensifying, his smile widening, his posture—well, he seemed to lean into me as I wrote.

I finished and slid the form back.

"Thank kew," he said.

He wobbled to the back of his cubicle, mouthing something. There, he sat and stared at my form, just gazed longingly into its non-existent eyes. There was a drawer next to the man. He pulled it out and took out some sort of bib and tied it around his neck, then carried the form to a small table set as if for lunch, with a plate, silverware, and a cup for coffee. He placed the form on the plate and sat down.

From there, I really can't remember whether what I saw was real, but I heard a chomp and a rip.

The man took a bite out of my form. He was chewing it, all the time demonstrating surprisingly good table manners—elbows off the table, napkin on lap.

With his knife and fork, he cut the rest of the form into small bites. He speared one and slipped it into his mouth and chewed, smiling, yet chewing with his mouth closed as one should.

"Oh, I almost forgot," he said and bent down to a phonograph beneath the table. He lowered a needle onto a spinning record—Vivaldi's Four Seasons. Yes, vinyl is back. The music swelled as he continued his meal.

I rang the bell. "Excuse me," I said. "Excuse me. I'd like to renew my driver's license. Please?"

The man grunted and pushed himself away from his table. He shuffled to the drawer beneath the counter and brought out a form.

"Here, fill this out," he said and slid it to me along with a purple pen . . . and went back to his meal.

I filled out that form five times before I got my new license.

You Can Never Be Sure:
A Story of Love
by Jerry

THAT was it.
She was done with him.
Yet there he was with those big moony eyes.
Those big moony eyes that said love me.
Ohwhatthehell . . .

She beckoned to him.
And that's all it took, an invitation.
He followed her home.
No conversation.
This was, yes, this was love.

He sashayed after her, upstairs to her apartment and
on inside where he planted
the biggest, warmest kiss upon her, his paws on her
chest.

She rewarded him.
Oh, how she rewarded him.
She cast her gaze at her bedroom, the door slightly
ajar, disappeared for a while,
and returned in the filmiest of negligees.
He panted at the sight.

She motioned for him to come with her
into the kitchen
where she indeed did reward him
with a bowl of kibble.

March

Mr. Harvard goes to Yale
by John

I woke one March morning to find that I was trapped in a Yale dormitory. A giant white Y hung from the ceiling of the room, and the place smelled of failure and diminished renown.

"The horror!" I shouted.

That woke my roommate.

He pushed himself up on one elbow and peered at me, his eyes bleary. "Whazza matter?" he asked, less than enthused.

I knew it. He didn't care about me. He's a Yale man.

"Look," I said, "I'm in the wrong place. I have to get back to Harvard."

He stared, unsure what to say and finally said what anyone would have said in that moment: "Go back to sleep."

His head hit the pillow, and I sat up straighter, wondering how on earth I got here. I didn't remember being inebriated last night nor did I recollect going on some sort of 'trip.' I did remember falling asleep in my Harvard room and the next thing I knew, here I was.

Nothing made sense.

"Excuse me," I said, "I don't mean to bother you, but do you remember how I got here last night?"

He mumbled something.

"Please," I said, "just tell me how I got here."

He sighed, his eyes still closed. "Like any normal person, you opened the door, fell into bed and began to snore. Like you do every night."

I could tell from his tone that, if I said one more word, he was going to throw something at me. Yale men, uncivilized swine. Never willing to settle a debate in a gentlemanly fashion.

I stayed there, trying to remember anything, but there was absolutely nothing worth remembering. I had an exam, took it yesterday feeling quite pleased with myself afterwards. I had lunch at The Investors Club, like I did every Tuesday, and I studied in the evening, like I did every evening. There was just nothing out of the ordinary except this: waking up in Yale.

"I've got to get out of here," I muttered and got up. I found my shoes next to my bed which is normally where I put them. I stepped into them, minus socks, and stood in front of a mirror next to the dresser...

I shrieked.

My roommate bounced up. He threw himself out of bed and slammed me against the wall. "What's the deal, man? Are you trying to make trouble or something?"

"I'm not supposed to be here. I'm not supposed to sleep here. I don't know who you are, and I'm definitely not supposed to be wearing this!" I gestured down at the big 'Y' on my sweatshirt that also had GO BULLDOGS printed on it. "I'm a crimson man. There has to be some mistake!"

The roommate broke off his stare. "I don't have time for this," he said as he went searching for his trousers. "But you do go to Yale. You've been my roommate for the entire year, and you're the biggest bulldog fan I know. Now what is wrong with you?"

"I'm a crimson man!"

Nothing seemed to be registering with him. Not unusual for a Yale man.

"I've got to get out of here," I said.

"Then go!"

And he helped me. He whipped open the door.

I ran through the doorway and down the hallway, jumping over masses of beer cans and bottles. I grabbed someone coming out of a room. "How do I get out of here?" I yelled.

He stared at me like I was some kind of wild man, yet he pointed ahead. "That way, then down the stairs two flights."

I broke away and ran. On the stairs I came on another student, this one drunk, bellowing the Bulldog fight song.

I flipped him off.

I rammed through the door at the bottom of the stairwell and ran out . . . into the middle of the campus, into clusters of students shouldering book bags, on their way to classes. I raced away from them to a street and flagged down a car.

The driver rolled down his window. "Can I help you?" he asked.

'Yes, please, I need a ride to Harvard!"

"Well, lucky duck, man, I'm headed in that

direction."

I threw myself into the passenger seat. "Thank you," I said, "thank you so much."

I was so relieved and suddenly so exhausted. The seat was so comfortable, so soft, the car so warm that I nodded off. Next time I wake up, I thought, I'll be in Harvard.

SOMEONE SHOOK ME. "Hey," a voice said, "we're here."

I opened my eyes, excited at the thought of being back where I belonged, but, as I gazed out the window, nothing looked familiar.

"Where are we?" I asked.

"Princeton."

The Letter
by Jerry

*Note: This story is my entry in the Ogle-Winnebago Literary Society's short story contest. The writing prompt for the entries was "This is the only story I'll ever tell" or the only story that one of my characters will ever tell. The story length required was 1,500 to 3,000 words. My story came in about midway between the extremes.

The Letter

THE OLDER MAN laid his arm across the younger's shoulders, both men in dark suits and ties expected for a funeral, their boots buffed to a high gloss, their collars turned up against the prairie wind. "I've got something for you," the older said.

The younger, his eyes dewy and his hair flicking this way and that, poked at the sod with the toe of his boot, the sod not yet greened up. "We just put my dad in the ground. I really ought to stay with my mom."

"Your sister can do that. Look, I was your father's

lawyer. This is important."

"I suppose." The younger wagged a finger at a young woman in a storm coat closer to the still open grave, his finger directing her toward an older woman in black, silver strands streaking her hair, the woman dabbing at her eyes with the corner of a silk handkerchief.

He got a nod in return, so moved away, off to the side of the funeral party and under a maple bare of leaves. He and the older man stopped, quarter to one another.

The older planted his cattleman's hat on his head, then drew an envelope from the inside pocket of his suit coat. "I've had this letter in my safe for a month. It's from your father. His instruction to me was to give it to you after he died."

"After he killed himself, you mean."

"That's the way it turned out, yes. I'm sorry." He held the envelope up. "I really think you should read this."

"Now?"

"Your father said it's important."

The younger took the envelope. "Do you know what's in the letter?"

"No."

He tore the end off the envelope and blew into it the way he had seen his father open envelopes so many times. The sides puffed out, and he reached in with two fingers for the folded paper. He snapped the paper open and read, the only sound around him that of the restless wind:

February 12, 2016

My son --

If you're reading this, I'm dead.

Forgive me for having made a fast exit. Getting help from the V.A. has been damn hard, such long waits for appointments with the shrinks. To them, rank means nothing. And when your head, pardon me, my head is all screwed up . . .

I was career Army, as you know -- 20 years. And you know the highlights, the good stuff. The early and late years were good. But the middle years, one year in particular, one three-month period, late September 2001 to December . . .

I've never told your mother this or you or your sister Gwenny, but for those months I was in Afghanistan, one of two dozen Green Berets and how many CIA guys I don't know charged with leading the Afghan Northern Alliance in their drive to rid the country of the Taliban. We Green Berets all spoke Farsi, fluent Farsi. That's why we were selected.

We rode in on two Chinook Nightstalkers flying so damn high to get over the Hindu Kush Mountains that we all had to suck on bottles of oxygen or we would have died. I shared my O-2 with my war dog, Werbly. I know, it's a sissy name for an almost fully black German shepherd that would rip someone's leg off when ordered, so I called him Wolf. After eleven hours in the air, the chopper crew put us down in some farmer's field in the Dari-a-Souf Valley at O-Two-Hundred. It was just thirty-nine days after Nine-Eleven, and we boiled out of our chopper ready for a fight, but there was no one. We had to walk for a day and a half before we came on a couple guys on horseback, scouts, it turned out, for the Northern Alliance army.

We had three-million dollars with us, cash money in hundred-dollar bills with which to buy the loyalty of the warlords, crates of money that we slung between us on our march. Damn lucky we didn't walk into a Taliban ambush. Had we, we might have ended up making the enemy rich.

The Taliban -- the T-Men, that's what we called them -- were as bad as bad men come, bandits and killers, and they still are. Those T-Men of my generation conquered their country in the name of Allah, they said, took it after the Ruskies pulled out and after seven years of civil war. They established Sharia law. Harsh law. Terrible law. They would cut off your hand or kill you for breaking it. If you've never read up on Sharia, you should. Just google it.

Most of us in my unit, the 595 -- the Army's Operational Detachment Alpha 595 -- and our sister unit, the 555, dressed like Afghanis, robes over our desert camos. Some of us had full beards and long hair, and half or more of us wore pakols, the soft, round-topped hats that Afghani men wear. We lived like the Afghanis with the Afghanis. We rode horses everywhere, a hell of an experience for me, a towny, because the only time I ever rode a horse was on the merry-go-round with you and Gwenny when you were little kids. But in the mountain north, horses are the only way to get around.

We were the cavalry.

We could and did move fast with our Northern Alliance brothers, 10 to 30 klicks a day.

I got the thrill of a lifetime -- actually, I thought I was going to die -- when we were picking our way down a mountainside on switchback trails sometimes only a foot wide. My horse must have decided he'd had enough because he turned in the trail, faced down the mountain, crouched like a cat, and sprang into the air. He must have flown 20 feet down the mountain before his hooves hit the ground and then he raced the rest of the way down like someone had jammed an electric prod up his butt and lit him up. All I could think to do was lay back, whip my feet up by his neck, and hang on. At the bottom, that wild stallion leaped across a gully and, apparently pleased with himself, stopped. Shaking, I slid off the saddle and kissed the ground. I really did.

It was the better part of a half an hour before the rest of the 595's and Wolf came off that mountain and caught up with me. I got a new nickname out of it: Rodeo . . . Rowdy "Rodeo" Gurnholt. No longer was I "Gurney," the nickname you'd have got tagged with had you joined the Army.

Rodeo. Sometimes Rodie.

Most of the battles we engaged in were small ones -- firefights -- but there were two massed assaults. In October, the General -- what was his name, Dostrum? Can you believe it, that's Afghani. -- he led 1,500 Northern Alliance horse soldiers and an equal number of ground pounders against the T-Men dug in at Bishqab. The T-Men had a couple tanks, several anti-aircraft guns, and a half-dozen APCs -- armored personnel carriers -- all of them bristling with cannons and machine guns, a lot of killing power . . . and us with just horses and M-16s. Well, we had a surprise for them, a couple forward air controllers who called in a squadron of F-16 Falcons.

They pounded the town with missiles and bombs.

Still we had to ride across a mile of open ground to get at the Taliban. From the air, it must have looked like Picket's Charge or the Charge of the Light Brigade. We made it, but we lost fourteen Northern Alliance fighters in the charge. Without the 16's, it would have been in the hundreds, maybe a thousand or more.

The next day we rode against Cobaki and overran the T-Men again. So much killing in two days, we of them.

We had been told we would be in Afghanistan a year, but after three months, the Taliban we didn't kill fled to Pakistan.

Good riddance.

Our job was done.

But we lost some, too, outside of those two big fights and the small ones. The suicide bombers who are creating so much hell now, I saw them first in Afghanistan. When we had the T-Men on the run, they turned loose the fanatics willing to blow themselves up if it meant they could kill us and the Afghanis we led. We got good fast at spotting the men, so they sent in the women, and that we never expected.

One, coming from a market with a big basket of produce and fruit, offered to sell what she had to a claque of our allies. She had five armed men around her, bargaining, haggling, when she set off her explosive belt. Cut herself in half and killed those five.

I saw it. God, I was a witness to it -- the slaughter, the carnage. That night, we of the 595 gathered behind the mud walls of a compound and agreed we'd never let that happen to us, that we would kill any women in burkas who came at us, who would not stop when we ordered them to do so.

Two days later, a little Afghani woman ran at us. She ran from a couple with whom she was walking, ran straight at us, and I had to cut her down. I killed her with a burst from my M-203 because she wouldn't stop.

Only she wasn't a woman. When we got her face covering off -- her face veil -- we saw she was only a kid, a girl maybe 12 or 13. And she didn't have a bomb or a suicide belt.

A girl not yet a teenager.

I threw up my guts.

One of our 595's got the couple aside. They had been yelling at us in Farsi not to shoot and now they were wailing, grief stricken. He asked who was she? And the man, in a rage of anger, shouted she was his daughter. She was deaf. She saw Wolf -- loved dogs -- and only wanted to pet him, that she was impulsive. She could not hear us or her parents.

That girl, Tom, she haunts me to this day. At night, that's when it's the worst. Try as I might, I have not been able to shake her from my mind. And I've tried it all -- Oxy, whiskey, head docs, and more Oxy. The stuff's easy to get if you know who to ask.

Three months into the war, the diplomats set up a civilian government, and we were ordered out of the country, ordered back to our bases, the 595's to our base in the Kuwaiti desert. Wolf was killed there. We were playing catch with a frisbee. Once he ran out for it and triggered a land mine left from the first Iraq war. The engineers had missed it. There was nothing, absolutely nothing to bury, not even his collar. I cried the rest of the day and all that night.

Suck it up, they tell you. Sometimes you can't.

The civilian Afghan government turned out to be no better than the Taliban. They were really corrupt, stealing everything they could. So the Taliban returned.

But that wasn't the 595's concern. We were out of there. We had done our job. Others screwed it up.

While we were there, Tommy, we snatched what comfort we could where we could. I took a bullet in one firefight and had to lay out a couple weeks. A family lived in the hut where the Northern Alliance put me. They conscripted the hut and ordered the family to take care of me. We became friends in time, laughing a lot about the silliest things. And the girl -- well, young woman . . . you know where this is going and why I've never told this story to anyone. I loved her, I really did. You've never been in a war, so I know you can't understand how that could happen in so short a time. Nine, ten months later, I got a letter from the head man, telling me that I had fathered twins. Tom, you have two sisters you never knew about.

I couldn't get them. I couldn't get their mother. By then some crazed uncle had killed her, her father wrote. An honor killing. There was no honor in that. I had family here -- you and Gwenny and your mother -- so I arranged to send the man and his wife money, so much a month so they could take care of their grandbabies -- my babies -- because the family had so little. And I've done that every month since for 14 years now.

You will find in my will that you have an inheritance. I want you to do

one of two things for me with that
money, either continue to support my
Afghani girls where they are or go
bring them home and adopt them. Ten
years and they could be through
college and on their own.

The first, Tom, that's not asking
much. The second, I know that's asking
you to do what I could not force
myself to do but should have. You're a
good son, Tom. I trust you. Be
stronger than I was.

Now what you choose to tell your
mother, well, that's your decision.
Just know that I will not be hurt.

Because I'm dead.

Dad

He folded the letter.

"Well?" the older man asked.

The younger looked away, across the rows of
headstones, to the hearse leaving the cemetery. He
raked his fingers back through his blowing hair.
"Dammit. Dammit to hell, I'm gonna have to go to
Afghanistan."

April

April's Story
by John

IN THIRD GRADE, April had a crush on a boy named George, the tallest boy in class, and he could run really fast. It was almost spring break, and the kids were ready for their vacations. We all sat around and our teacher, Mrs. Bennett, asked us about our plans.

Bethany said she was going to California, to Disneyland.

John said he was off to Six Flags.

Lisa, not enthusiastic, stared at the floor. "I'm gonna be home with my parents. Boring," she said.

April said she was going to stay home, too. What she didn't say was that she hoped George would, too, that maybe they might have a play date on a Sunday afternoon. They were, after all, next-door neighbors, but they never talked. April had fallen in love with George after the school play where he was the pig, a part he played, she thought, to perfection.

I know April. She's shy. She can talk with her mother and father just fine, but anyone outside the family circle, that's difficult. She had been trying to build up the courage to talk to George for a long time, and she wanted this spring break to be a kind of springboard for building a relationship with him.

Mrs. Bennett came to me, and I said I was just going to stay home.

"Very nice," she said with sweet intentions. "And how about you, George? What are you doing this spring break?"

George sat up, excited. "I'm going to Disney World," he said, "in Florida."

We all gasped. We were jealous.

For April, Disney World would put George a long way away from her, and she slumped in her chair, probably thinking better luck next year.

THAT FRIDAY before spring break hit, I saw April moping around the playground. A lot of the kids from our school had gone home early, to get a head start on their trips, I guess. George, though, was still here, playing on the monkey bars with his crew, playing hot lava.

April must have been thinking maybe she could talk to him before he goes because she picked herself up and headed towards the monkey bars, nervous it looked like to me because, for every two steps she took forward, she took one back.

"I can do this," I heard her say with every step she took. "I can do this. I like him and he should know it."

She got closer and closer to the monkey bars, and when she was just about there—

BRRRRING!

The bell.

And all of us ran inside except April.

George and his gang raced each other, insulting each other on the way in. "I'm gonna beat you, you slow poke," George shouted to his counterpart, but it seemed like he was shouting to April. As he passed her, she gave him a big smile and ran inside, too.

THE SCHOOL DAY ended and everyone left, excited with what spring break was about to bring them. Everyone, except April and me. I wasn't in any hurry. She dragged herself outside to her parents, and, just as she got near them, I saw her gaze at George standing alone, waiting for his parents.

She stopped. I guess she wanted to talk to him, but it must have been too much.

George, though, looked at her and smiled. "Hi," he said.

"Oh, hi," she said. But she said it so softly I wondered whether he had heard her.

He had.

"You're April, right?" he asked.

"Yeah, and you're George." She smiled, and it must have felt like a million suns were burning in her cheeks.

Her father waved to her. "Hey, April! We're over here, darling."

"Coming, Dad."

But she continued to gaze at George. "So, you're going to Disney World?" she asked.

"Yeah. And you? You're staying here?"

"Yeah, just me and my parents."

"That's not too bad," he said. "They seem really cool."

That's when I saw his parents pull up in their SUV. "My mom and dad," he said. "I'll see you later, April."

George trotted to the car and stuffed his backpack in the backseat.

And April walked away, but I saw her glance back as George said to his parents, "That girl, she talked to me!"

She smiled for the second time that day, and it was a glittering smile.

Digging in the Dirt
by Jerry

ALEX DENLY licked his index finger and held it high.

Nothing.

He turned ninety degrees, still holding his finger up.

Nada.

No wind.

Not even a springtime breeze.

Temperature sixty-five.

Soil dry.

A great day to spade up a garden.

Denly headed to the garage at the far corner of the backyard for a shovel and a garden rake. The garage, home for his 'Eighty-seven Dodge Raider–he'd restored it himself and put on oversized mud tires– and his wife's Chevy Volt, had been a carriage house when the Brinkmann Mansion was the social center for the town's Elite Ten–the ten richest families–back at the turn of the century.

The last century.

The Denlys bought the crumbling old dowager last fall for little more than the tax bill on orders from the county to either fix it up or pull it down. Denly figured if he could restore a truck, he could restore a house, that it shouldn't be much harder, just take more money, money he and his wife had.

He tossed the shovel and rake in a wheelbarrow, and trundled them outside to an area next to the garage that had once been a garden, but had become, like the house, a ruin. He figured to turn over the soil, smooth it some, and plant the cool-weather vegetables–radishes, carrots, lettuce, a few beets, and maybe a kohlrabi or two–before day's end.

He chunked the spade into the soil and turned over the first clump and . . . what was that?

Denly leaned down. With his fingers, he excavated something that was longer than his thumb, a bit thin, yet lumpy. He worked the lumps off and much of the rest of the dirt.

Riley Denly came up behind him with a glass of sweet tea. She glanced over his shoulder. "Find some magnificent treasure there, sweetcakes?"

"Maybe. Oh, I don't know." He took a bandana from his back pocket and rubbed the item clean, then held it up. "Whaddaya think?"

"A skeleton key?"

"Looks like it, doesn't it."

She put her hand on his arm. "Remember those old Nancy Drew books, the really old ones that were my grandmother's? In them, Nancy was always finding skeleton keys that would open something or other and solve the mystery. Wonder what this opens?"

"My bet, the house." Denly hopped the key in his hand. "Someone probably lost it out here when they were picking beans one day."

He pocketed the key and went back to turning over the soil. On the sixth or seventh spadeful–he wasn't counting—he turned up a small disc that looked to be about the size of a quarter. Denly picked it out of the dirt and began cleaning it, his wife watching as she swirled her tea in her glass. The more he rubbed, the more the color changed from dirt black to . . .

"Is that gold, sweets?" she asked.

He took her glass and poured tea over the disc and rubbed it clean with his bandana. Finished, he studied one side of the disc, then the other. "A ten-dollar gold piece, a Liberty minted in Eighteen Ninety-nine. Hon, this'll get us dinner and drinks at Applebee's."

"Maybe more." She brought out her cell and googled 'gold coins, U.S. denominations.' "There's a site here that says that's worth just under—get this—seven hundred dollars."

"I guess we're gonna have lots of nights out."

"Do you suppose there are more?"

"Wait here." Denly trooped back to the garage and returned with a metal detector that had been his father's. For him, all it had found were some square nails, a handle from a tin cup, a few old pennies, and a corroded horseshoe.

Denly snapped the power switch on. As the detector hummed up, he adjusted the sensitivity settings and commenced sweeping the area. "This screen," he said, motioning at a digital readout, "if I get a really strong hit, this should tell me how deep the object is, how much digging I'm gonna have to do."

Riley Denly followed along, watching the

readout.

An alarm sounded.

Denly peered at the screen and gave off a pained look. "Trash. Could be a wad of tinfoil."

He went on, stepping away from the garage toward the lawn, sweeping the detector over the ground. The readout jumped. "A ring maybe? It's junk metal, at least that's the indication."

He swivelled ninety degrees, toward the back fence. A new alarm sounded, more high-pitched this time and louder. Denly tapped a command that changed the readout. "This is big, hon."

Riley Denly glanced at her husband.

"And deep. At least three feet." He laid the detector aside and went back for his spade.

FROM DEEP in the hole, Denly struck something. He hunkered down and pawed the dirt away. "Rye?"

She leaned out over the hole, her shadow enveloping him.

"I think I've got a metal box down here. Get me a whisk broom from the garage, wouldja?"

"Anything for you, my darling one," she said and meandered away.

He straightened up and tapped with the point of his spade, feeling for the edge of the box. He found it and began excavating, pitching the dirt up and out of the hole. Twenty minutes and he had enough of one side and an end exposed that he knew he'd dug deeper than the box. "Rye," he called up, "I need a trowel."

Again she disappeared.

While he waited, he took the whisk broom he'd stuffed in his back pocket and brushed away dirt from the top, side, and end of the box, as much as he could, uncovering in the process some fixtures on the box. Using the length of his hand for reference, he estimated the dimensions of the box, and they suggested that—

It can't be, he thought.

"Catch," Riley called to him.

He looked up, his face dirt smeared, and caught the trowel. "Rye, hon, I think we've got a child's casket here."

"In the garden?"

"I don't believe it, either."

Denby troweled out handholds under the box. He fitted his fingers into them and lifted, but the box refused to give. He lifted again and something in his back popped. Denly leaned back against the side of the hole, grimacing, raking the sweat from his forehead with his sleeve. "Rye?"

"Yes?"

"Remember that short spud bar I have in the garage?"

"I remember everything you have in the garage. Maybe I should bring it all."

"Just the spud bar. And before you go, any iced tea left in your glass?"

"Some."

"Hon, I've got a heckuva thirst."

She handed him the glass and departed.

He guzzled the tea down to the ice cubes, one of which he took out and rubbed over the back of his neck.

She came back toting the bar, and he rammed it under the box and pried up. No give. He rammed the bar under a second place and lifted. Still no give.

A third time he rammed the bar under, and when he hauled up on it, the hard-packed dirt beneath the box released its hold. Denly threw the bar aside. He squatted down and wrestled the box into his arms, pushed himself up and shoved the box out to the side of the hole. He did a 'gimme' motion at the spud bar.

Riley handed the tool to him, and he broke open the lock with it.

Denly lifted the cover back.

She peered inside. "We need to call the police."

He, too, peered into the box. "Damn. Gimme your cell. It's the sheriff we need to call. We're in the county."

HOWARD ZIGMAN, lead detective for the Wappello County Sheriff's Department, hovered over the shoulder of the county's medical examiner, Akeema Stennard, she in her lab whites kneeling on a tarp at the side of the box.

Stennard prodded at the bones. "Have to be from a child," she said.

"How old?"

"Hard to tell. I can reassemble them back in the morgue and do some measurements. I can give you an idea then."

"Any way to know how long they've been here?"

"Not with any certainty." She brought out some

bits of fabric from the casket and rubbed it between her fingers. "Feels like silk."

"So?"

"Casket manufacturers haven't used silk to line their caskets for a long time. They use polyester now and probably have since around Nineteen Fifty." Stennard sat back on her heels. She looked up at Zigman. "Detective–"

"Call me Howard."

"All right. Howard, I did my graduate work up at the U.W. They've got carbon-dating equipment there. They could run tests for us. They could give us a good estimate."

"How good?"

"Within a five-year range."

Zigman shrugged and stepped away onto the grass. There he raked the dirt from his Nunn Bush shoes onto the sod. "What I'd really like to know is who this child is."

"There's a slim chance I can get a DNA sample from one of the bones. If I can, that will tell us whether it's a girl or a boy."

"Yes. Yes, you do that." Zigman, his ever-present leather notecase under his arm, moved off to the Denlys sitting at a shaded picnic table, a hibachi out and ready for the grilling season. He sat down and there laid open his notecase. "Strange way to start your day, isn't it?"

Denly leaned his chin on his hands folded together, his elbows propped on the table. "If I hadn't got out my dad's metal detector, we wouldn't have known."

"Metal detector?"

"Yes. I was digging up the garden and I found this key and this coin—" He laid them on the table. "—so I thought I ought to see if there was anything else of interest."

Zigman, with his pen, pulled the key toward himself. "This is an oldie."

"Probably goes to the house. Who knows how long ago someone dropped it out here while weeding or checking the sweet corn."

Zigman pulled over the coin. He took a magnifying glass from his jacket's inside pocket and studied the coin. "I've got a cousin who's into things like this if you want to have it appraised."

"Rye's already looked it up on the internet."

"Of course." Zigman returned the coin and clicked his pen, ready to write. "You moved in here when?"

"October." Denly took hold of his wife's hand. "Rye and I launched a dot com out on the West Coast a couple years ago, went nuts building it. So we sold out to move back closer to home—to get away from the pressure."

Riley smiled. "Alex always had this dream of owning a little newspaper. The weekly came up for sale here, and we bought it and the house."

"But that was a separate thing, the house," Denly said.

Zigman jotted some words while he watched Denly. "Know anything about the history of the place? That may help me figure out who buried the child."

"The history? Just what the realtor told us."

Riley leaned in. "A Mister Otto Brinkmann–Brinkmann, 'mann' with two n's–built the house for his wife. Her name was Heidi, I think. The year the realtor said was Eighteen Ninety-eight."

"Brinkmann," Denly said, "made his fortune buying and selling land."

Riley nodded. "They had two children–girls. We really don't know what happened to them. The Brinkmanns lived here until they died. I think she said Mister Brinkmann died in Nineteen Forty-one, his wife the year after."

Denly tapped on the table top. "There were a half-dozen owners in the intervening years, none with the money to keep the place up. So here we are."

"Yes, here we are." Zigman finished his notes. He closed his notecase and got up, as if to leave. "You called the sheriff, not nine-one-one. Why?"

Denly looked up. "I know the sheriff through Rotary. This wasn't an emergency, so it seemed the right way to go."

"You didn't do anything more than open the casket, did you?"

"No."

"You didn't take pictures?"

"Well, yes, with Rye's cell, for the story I have to write. I own a newspaper."

"Yes, you said." Zigman got out his business card and handed it on. "Forward all your picture files to my cell, would you, please? They could prove helpful."

ZIGMAN DRIFTED into The Library, a favorite bar in downtown Jamestown, odd for the strongest drink Zigman ever ordered was a Cherry Coke. He waved to the bartender, Barb Larson, and made his way to a back booth where three others were seated—Zigman's sounding board when he came on a particularly puzzling case, snoops ready to assist in gathering information, grist for a detective.

Each glanced up in turn from the Scrabble board in front of them—Ethel Hall, senior reference librarian at the city library; Rand Farquare, retired sports editor for the Jamestown Daily Enterprise, called The Cracker—short for Firecracker—by his closest friends; and Farquare's wife, Maredith, who headed up the local garden club—the Flower City Iris And Orchid Society.

"You're late," The Cracker said.

Zigman slid in beside Hall. "Long day and a conversation with the sheriff almost as long."

"About those bones you found out at the Brinkmann place?"

"You heard?"

"Channel Three had the story."

"Then you know I didn't find the bones. Alexander Denly did."

"The guy who owns our weekly, yes. So?"

Three sets of eyes focused on Zigman.

"All right. The sheriff wants me to chuck the case, throw the file in the bottom drawer of my desk."

"But you've hardly started investigating," Hall said.

"His point is we don't know who the child is and have no way of finding out, that the child died more than sixty-five years ago under what circumstances we don't know, and whoever may have been involved is probably dead. Move on, he says, you've got more pressing cases that need your time and the department's budget."

Maredith Farquare looked at her husband, then Zigman. "Do you?"

"You want me to list them for you?"

"Of course not."

"It's just that I can't let any case go without at least trying a little bit to figure it out."

Hall ran a finger around the rim of her empty wine glass. "All right, how can we help?"

Barb Larson came hustling by with a Cherry Coke and three glasses of Northleaf Zinfandel, one of them a fourth glass for Hall who had started early. Larson gathered all the empty glasses on the table onto her tray and swept away to a new party waiting inside the door.

Zigman clicked his glass against Hall's. "How about you spending some time in the Wappello Room and see if you can put together a history on the Brinkmanns. They lived there the longest in the time period I'm concerned about."

"You think the child could be theirs?"

"Or a hired girl's or a cousin's or I don't know. I just need anything and everything you can find on the family."

The Cracker sipped from his glass. He sipped again and gave off with a mellow smile. "This is pretty good stuff. You'd never guess it's from a winery just down the road. Zig, tell you what, I'll go into the newspaper office in the morning and dig out the obits of the Brinkmanns. Those may tell us something. If there are any descendants, maybe Mare and I can track 'em down for you."

Akeema Stennard came in the door of The Library in her off-duty wear—jeans and a Willie Nelson & Family 2016 Tour tee-shirt. She stopped at the bar and, after a few words with Larson, picked up a Spotted Cow and came on to Zigman's booth, jacking the cap off the bottle with the opener on her Swiss army knife. Stennard hooked her boot around the leg of a chair and dragged it over.

Zigman gazed at her as she sat down. "You know everybody here?"

"Uh-huh, your posse."

"So what brings you by?"

She sucked down a quarter of her beer and, as she set the bottle down, exhaled an ahh. "This is what got me through med school, beer and friends who didn't care a whit what I was studying. But why I'm here. The sheriff told me to shut down my work on your Baby Doe case."

Zigman turned up a palm. "He told me the same."

"Only I didn't. I got a DNA sample off to the state crime lab with a note that they were to send the report to me and no one else." She sucked down more of her bottle's contents, down to the half-way mark–half way down the label. "Now remember, you didn't hear any of this from me."

"What else didn't I hear?"

"I sifted through the stuff in the bottom of the casket, and I found this." Stennard brought out a tissue-wrapped object from her pocket. She peeled the tissue back. "A locket."

Zigman took it from Stennard's hand. He felt along the locket's edge for the catch that would release the cover, found it and opened the locket.

Maredith Farquare twisted the locket toward her. She gazed at the picture it contained, a picture of a young woman with a demure smile, her face ringed by a halo of dark hair. "Do you think this could be the child's mother?"

"And there's one thing more," Stennard said. "In examining the bones, I found a fracture in the child's skull, not terribly prominent. But I can't help wondering, how did it get there?"

ZIGMAN WASN'T MUCH for public speaking, but when Maredith Farquare asked him to provide a program for the AARP meeting at the Jamestown Senior Center, she had him in a box. It was that one-hand-washes-the-other thing.

"The most puzzling case I think I've ever had," he said to the silver hairs seated before him, "is the one I have now that, because of time and budget constraints, I can't pursue. Yesterday, the owners of the Brinkmann place at the edge of town found a child's casket buried in their garden. It may have been there sixty-five years, probably more. Now who is the child? Why was the child buried there? How did the child come to die? If there ever was a cold, cold, cold case, this is going to be it because the sheriff has decided we don't have the time, manpower or budget to pursue it. And, sadly, I have to say he's right. Well, thank you for listening to me. And remember, this is an election year, so please, when you step into the voting booth, vote for my sheriff."

Soft laughter rippled through the room.

Maredith Farquare rose from her chair beside the podium and led the audience in applause. "I want to thank Detective Zigman for coming," she said. "Why don't we adjourn to coffee and brownies that Mildred Fenwell has made and you can talk to the detective there?"

Zigman touched her arm. "I really have to go."

"Zig, one brownie, one question, you can do that much."

He sighed and trudged away after Farquare to the dessert table. There, as he lifted a double-chocolate walnut and craisins brownie onto a napkin, a small woman, her face as deeply lined as a prune, tugged at his sleeve. Zigman glanced her way.

"Detective Zigman," she said, "I'm Missus Arnold Hendershot. I grew up next door to the Brinkmann place. My mother, rest her soul, knew them well, particularly the children because the youngest was about her age. They were best friends, she said."

"Really?"

"Do you remember those heart lockets that came with a small key—the key to my heart?"

"I've seen pictures."

"My mother and Sophia–that's Sophia Brinkmann–they bought two heart lockets, identical, made of pewter, at the Woolworth Five-and-Dime. In Sophia's, they put a picture of my mother, and in my mother's, they put a picture of Sophia. Would you like to see it?"

MISSUS HENDERSHOT TOOK hold of Zigman's hand as he helped her out of his car. "You know," she said, smiling up at him, "I was a little worried when you offered to give me a ride home."

"Worried? About what?"

"That my neighbors would see me, you know, getting out a police car, and I'd have to explain to them that I wasn't picked up for shoplifting at the Walmart again."

"Were you?"

They went up the front walk, Missus Hendershot clinging to Zigman's arm. "One time, but it was a misunderstanding."

"How was that?"

"The policeman let me off after I gave them back the New York strip steak that had fallen into my purse. Then he gave me a ride home. Thank goodness he didn't turn his lights on, but still it was a police car."

"Mine is unmarked. Your neighbors will never know who gave you a lift today."

"And I do thank you for that. Now do come inside."

She led the way into her Cape Cod bungalow. Zigman puttered around the living room, looking at family pictures on the wall and the piano, while Missus Hendershot went on to her bedroom.

"It should be in this jewelry box," she said as she returned, carrying a teakwood box inlayed with ivory. She opened it on the coffee table. "Would you like some tea? I always keep a kettle on the stove."

He put the edge of his hand to his chin. "I'm full up to here."

"Well, then–" Missus Hendershot poked a finger around through the contents of the jewelry box. "–I did see the locket in here, oh, I think it was perhaps five years ago." She held up a pearl bracelet, then an emerald broach, and finally a silver spoon on which was stamped World's Fair 1925 San Francisco.

"My father gave this to my mother. He was a merchant marine, and his ship had stopped in San Francisco. My mother always thought this spoon was so special." She went back to digging in the box. "Oh, yes, here it is."

She brought out a locket, a key attached to it and a chain streaming after it. She placed the locket in Zigman's hand.

Zigman brushed his fingertips over the locket, over the intricate tooling of a rose in the cover. He opened it. "May I borrow this?"

THE LOCKET NAGGED at Zigman as he drove back to the county's justice center, a refined name recommended by the architect for the complex that housed the sheriff's department, its auxiliary services, and the jail. Everyone else called it the Wappello Cop Shop & Lock-up. Zigman parked, left his car, and walked in to the duty board where he slid his name from the OUT column to the IN column. There, he saw, in the OUT column–the sheriff's name.

Excellent, he thought, and took the cargo elevator down to the basement, to the morgue and Stennard's office, the whole area smelling of cleaning agents and disinfectant. Zigman went in and found Stennard hunched over the keyboard of her computer, typing away.

He closed the door. "Akeema, I've got something that will interest you."

She turned away from her work, and he placed the Hendershot locket on her desk, in front of the medical examiner.

She peered at it.

"Open it."

Stennard did, surprise lighting her face. She touched the picture in the locket. "This is the same as the one in the locket I found in the casket, isn't it? Do you know who she is?"

"One of the Brinkmann girls–Sophia–according to the woman who's had this locket for the last forty-nine years."

Stennard lifted out several strands of hair. "Now this is an old-time practice, giving someone a lock of your hair."

"Girls did that back then, I'm told."

She motioned Zigman into a side chair. "So who did this Sophia give her hair to?"

"A girl about her age–Thelma Ritter. Her daughter, Missus Hendershot, had the locket. Says

Missus Hendershot, the Brinkmanns and the Ritters lived next door to one another, that her mother and Sophia Brinkmann were best friends growing up."

Stennard held up the strands of hair. "You're thinking this must be the Brinkmann girl's hair?"

"Has to be."

"I can send this to the crime lab and get a DNA profile of the family, at least one person in the family. This could be helpful. And speaking of DNA–" She turned her computer's screen to Zigman, tapped in several commands, and brought up a report from the state crime lab time/dated ten thirty-nine this morning. "I asked for a quick-and-dirty–is the sample male or female?"

Zigman massaged his lower lip as he scanned down the screen, his gaze moving from paragraph to paragraph. He shook his head.

Stennard aimed her ballpoint at Zigman. "Yes, it's a boy. And my measurements of the bones suggest it was perhaps a couple weeks old to maybe three months."

She turned the screen back and cleared it. "Do you want my theory of the parentage?"

Zigman shrugged. "Theories are just that, theories."

Stennard took an evidence envelope from her desk drawer. She placed the hair strands in the envelope, sealed it, and wrote her notes on the cover. "This Brinkmann girl is the mother. Why else would a locket with her picture be in the casket?"

She held up the envelope. "Now if this hair is hers, we should be able to compare the DNA profile from the hair with the DNA profile from the bones. If half, say, of forty-five markers in the hair's sample are in the bone's sample, we've got the mother."

ZIGMAN LOUNGED in his booth at The Library playing Jeopardy on his cell, a Cherry Coke at his elbow.

Larson slipped in beside him, bumping his hip. "Winning biggety big time, Zig Man?"

"I was until I got to the mixed-drink mixology category."

"You should have called me over."

Zigman, an eyebrow raised, peered to his side, at Larson. She sensed his coolness and slipped out of the booth as his posse crowded in.

The Cracker waggled three fingers at Larson before she could disappear. "Wine, three times," he said. "We're up for adventure, so pick something we've never had before."

Larson fired a finger pistol at him and sauntered away, back to the bar.

The Cracker pulled a file folder from his satchel and slapped it on the table. "The Brinkmann family dossier."

He opened it and fanned out xerox copies of newspaper clippings.

Larson came back with a tray on which she carried three glasses and a wine bottle wrapped in a bar towel. She set the tray down and stabbed a corkscrew through the wax seal into the stopper and twisted away, watching the conversation.

The Cracker pushed one of the copies forward. "The obit for old man Brinkmann. He died in

Nineteen Forty-two, not 'Forty-one—March fifteenth, tax day to be exact, how about that?" He waited for a response. When none came, he went on. "Our Otto Bogohardt Brinkmann, age sixty-nine, left behind a wife, Heidi Kraus Brinkmann, and one daughter, Hanna, a resident of Madison, right here in our great state of brats, beer, and books."

Larson pulled the cork and poured a few drops into a glass. This she set in front of The Cracker. He sniffed the wine, indicating with a roll of his finger that she should fill the glasses.

"And the other daughter?" Zigman asked. "Sophia?"

The Cracker leaned back on the bench seat. He spread his hands. "No mention of a second daughter, not in Missus Brinkmann's obit either, nor in Hanna's obit which, incidentally, we found in The State Journal's electronic files with a google search."

He brought his glass up beneath his nose and inhaled the aroma. He gazed at Larson. "Delicious. Now what do we have here?"

"Let's see if you can figure it out."

The Cracker inhaled the aroma of the wine again. "I smell figs and cinnamon."

"Very good."

He sipped the wine. He did not swallow it, but let the liquid roll over his tongue, once and then a second time. And then he swallowed. "Raspberry? No, black raspberry. But this is a red wine, and sweet."

"So, you like it?"

"Barb, it's superb. Almost a dessert wine."

"Do you want to guess the vintner?"

"I couldn't."

The women raised their glasses. The Cracker, seeing that, touched his glass to theirs and they drank, the women nodding and smiling.

Larson let the bar towel fall away from the bottle, and The Cracker stared at the label. "The Oz Winery? Never heard of it."

She caressed the bottle. "Kansas–Wizard of Oz country. It's made in Wamego. That's west of Topeka. My dad got it for me, and a second bottle, when he went out there for a reunion of his company of the Big Red One."

The Cracker waggled his fingers at the bottle, and Larson gave it to him. He rubbed his hand over the label. "Yes, Wonderful Wizard of Oz Limited Edition. This I have to have for Mare. She collects all things Oz. How much?"

"A hundred and a quarter. Crack, that's dollars."

"Put it on Zig's tab."

Zigman popped his hand up like it was a stop sign.

The Cracker leaned in. "Zig, for what we're about to tell you, it's worth it."

Zigman looked up at the ceiling.

"It would appear," The Cracker said, toying with one of the copies, "from Hanna Brinkmann's obit that she was the end of the line. No children listed, and apparently she did not marry. She was an old-maid school teacher. Thirty-four years, the Catholic schools in Madison."

"Not helpful, Crack."

"Well, Mare and I got to wondering, since you told us there were two daughters, what happened to the other. We took that, since the other daughter was not mentioned in any of the Brinkmann obits, that she must have died a long time ago."

Maredith Farquare rubbed shoulders with her husband. "So I started thinking, what happened a long time ago? The answer that came to me is the great influenza epidemic of Nineteen Eighteen and Nineteen."

The Cracker covered his wife's hand with his. "The Spanish flu."

"More than fifty million people perished from it in our country, eight thousand right here in Wisconsin alone."

"So we went down to the courthouse and dug through the death records for Nineteen Eighteen, and there it was—"

Maredith Farquare went on with her husband's sentence. "A death certificate for a Sophia Brinkmann—the only Brinkmann we could find for that time period—so we knew it had to be the one we were looking for. She was twenty years old."

Ethel Hall cupped her wine glass in her hands. "Well, why wouldn't her mother have listed this Sophia child in her husband's obituary?"

"Or be listed in Hanna's obituary? It's a puzzle."

Zigman pulled over The Cracker's file. "I think there's something else going on here, and, if I'm right, Crack, it could well be worth that bottle of wine."

Zigman, in his car

in the dark
in an abandoned county rest stop,
sat leaning back, his eyes closed,
listening to Handel's *Solomon* on the radio,
directing the orchestra and chorus.

Lights in his mirror warmed his eyelids, but the lights winked out and Zigman continued to direct the music.

Someone opened the passenger door and slipped onto the seat.

Zigman sensed a faint aroma of perfume. The scent, the brand? He wasn't that good.

"Howard," a feminine voice said, "have you ever conducted an orchestra for real?"

Zigman let his fingers fall to the steering wheel. He turned his head toward his company, opening his eyes as he did. "Wouldn't that be nice? Whatcha got?"

Akeema Stennard, the county medical examiner, passed a file to Zigman. "You want to turn the volume down?"

"Of course." He punched the radio's volume control down several notches, until *Solomon* was little more than elevator music.

"If the sheriff saw us or heard of this—"

Zigman snapped the overhead light on and gazed at the file cover. "We're safe out here. The deputy who patrols this part of the county won't be by for—" He squinted at the clock in his car's dash. "—another twenty minutes or so."

Stennard touched the cover. "What you have here are the results of the latest DNA tests."

"Do you want me to look at the charts and be

befuddled?"

"Of course not. I'll give you the eight-word summary: Sophia is the mother of the dead baby."

"And the father?"

"That I don't know. Here's the rest of it. All of Sophia's DNA—one-hundred percent—is Germanic, and I expected that. What I didn't expect is that only seventy-five percent of the child's DNA is Germanic."

"And the other quarter?"

Stennard opened the file for Zigman. "African."

He pushed himself up straight and twisted toward Stennard.

"Yes, African," she said.

"How the . . . This county is as close to white bread as it can be. The first black family that I know of moved here back when I was in grade school. I went to school with one of the kids. Prior to that, nothing."

ZIGMAN WORKED his way into a file drawer in the Wappello Room, the drawer marked 'census records.' He fingered back through the folders to one on which someone had printed in a clear hand 1900.

This folder Zigman lifted out, along with folders for 1910 and 1920, and went to a study table.

There, under a lamp that gave extra light to the library's local history room, he paged into the 1900 folder, searching for the summary statement on race.

And found it.

On the line labeled Negroid, someone had pencilled in 3.

Zigman next dug into the 1910 and 1920 folders for the same summary statements. He pulled them out and laid them beside the first statement, so one could read across the three . . .

1900 Negroid, 3.

1910 Negroid, 3.

1920 Negroid, 0.

Zigman rubbed his face hard. He stretched the skin on his cheeks as he drew his hands down, wondering who these three were. What happened to them? Where did they go?

While he sat there cogitating, studying the tiles on the ceiling, the woman from the senior center made her way into the room in ever so measured steps. She stopped at Zigman's table. "Detective?"

"Huh? Oh." Zigman forced himself to focus on the woman–Missus Hendershot, still as short as she was, her face still as deeply lined.

"Detective, you looked to be lost there for a minute."

"Lost in puzzling."

"About what?"

He motioned her into the chair beside him and turned the three statements to her. "Missus Hendershot, when you were young, did you ever know of any black families to be in the county?"

"Not back then, but in my mother's time." She peered through her glasses at the 1910 statement. "You remember my mother and her siblings and their parents–my grandparents–they lived next door to the Brinkmanns. My mother told me they had servants– the Brinkmanns–a butler black as the ace of spades and a cook who was somewhat lighter."

"But the census says there were three."

"Oh, there were, detective. The Negroid couple had a boy that was a couple years older than my mother and Sophia Brinkmann. When the Brinkmanns had to go anywhere, my mother said, he would drive their car for them."

"Driving Miss Daisy?"

"Pardon?"

"Oh nothing."

"Does any of this help you?"

"Maybe, maybe not. I don't know. Would you like a lift home?"

ZIGMAN, MISSUS HENDERSHOT holding onto his arm, passed the circulation desk, heading for the exit when another woman hurried up—Ethel Hall, the library's senior reference librarian.

"Zig," she said, breathless, "I'm so glad I caught you before you got away."

He tipped his head toward Missus Hendershot, and Hall touched the woman's shoulder with both hands. "Gladys, you don't mind if I take the detective for a moment."

"Well, he has offered me a ride home."

"It'll just be for a minute."

Missus Hendershot smiled, the lines in her face lifting into crinkles, her eyes sparkling like sequins. She held out the book she had checked out, *Fifty Shades of Grey as Told by Christian*. "They say there's much more sex in this one. I'll just go over to the bench and bend a few pages while you two talk."

She shuffled away.

Hall nudged Zigman toward several overstuffed chairs by the plastic philodendron next to the 'returns' window.

After they settled into two, the chairs facing one another, Hall gazed at Zigman. "Zig, I've been working on a project, the KKK in Wappello County. It's for history month, and I found this."

She passed a folder to Zigman.

He looked at it, then turned it over. "Seems like everybody's got a folder these days."

Hall motioned for him to open it.

As he did, a yellowed newspaper clipping slipped out and see-sawed to the carpet. Zigman recovered the paper. Written at the top in pencil, Wisconsin State Journal and a date, October 27, 1922. Beneath it a headline, ATTORNEY GENERAL'S REPORT NAMES TRIPLE-K MEMBERS IN SOUTHERN WISCONSIN.

The story—six paragraphs and a list of names that filled two columns . . . names and towns. Zigman's gaze stopped on one—Otto Bogohardt Brinkmann, Jamestown.

"Holy moly."

Hall raised an eyebrow.

"He was a Klansman, and he employed a black family."

"Zig, what are you talking about?"

"I was looking through the census records in the Wappello Room, and we had three blacks in the county in Nineteen Hundred and Nineteen Ten, but none in Nineteen Twenty. And your friend, Missus

Hendershot over there, she told me that the Brinkmanns employed a family of three blacks as servants. How could Brinkmann do that if he was a Kluxzer?"

"Zig, maybe because he could. They were servants, as you say—subservient. Maybe, in his view, he was keeping them in their place."

"I've got to think about this. Can you call Crack and Maredith and we meet at The Library tonight? The other library?"

"And imbibe a little wine? Of course."

ZIGMAN, WITH STENNARD, made his way into bar and back to his booth, the posse already there, hunched over Moby Dick The Card Game, The Cracker rolling a die, a partially empty wine glass by each player.

The die stopped on a two, and The Cracker took a card from "The Sea" deck. He looked at it for a long moment before he threw it down face-up. "Dingly darn it all, I've hit a calm. I lose three turns."

Zigman hauled a chair over for himself while Stennard slipped onto the lone open space on one of the two bench seats. Zigman, as he sat down, gazed over the mess of cards and game chips. "Who wins at this?"

The Cracker, a pout on his face, crossed his arms. "The last player to survive."

"Now don't tell me. That player gets to be Ishmael, have I got it right?"

"Right."

"Can you take a break?"

The Cracker scratched at the stubble on his cheek. "Might as well. I'm not goin' anywhere for three turns."

Hall raised a finger. She waved it at Barb Larson as she came by and pointed at her near-empty glass. Larson gave her an okay and went on.

"Zig," Hall said, "you've figured it out, haven't you? Is this going to be like Hercule Poirot, he's got everyone in the room and he goes through the case, eliminating one suspect after another until there's only one left?"

"Something like that."

"I'm all ears."

Zigman pushed the cards back and opened his leather notecase on the table, the notecase containing his usual yellow pad plus four file folders. "All right, in these folders are several DNA reports, census summaries, and a number of newspaper clips along with my notes on each. Here's what I now know or at least feel sufficiently certain about."

He tapped his left index finger with his right. "Baby Bee—that's what our weekly newspaper publisher has named him—Baby Bee is Sophia's son. The DNA evidence supports that. The child was probably born out of wedlock, but that's a guess on my part."

Zigman touched the tip of the middle finger of his left hand. "A part of Baby Bee's DNA is African."

Maredith Farquare stared at Zigman.

"Mare, the Brinkmanns employed a black family as servants, the youngest member a boy—well, at this time a young man—a little older than Sophia. My guess is that young man is Baby Bee's father."

"Oh, come now."

"Mare, when you were eighteen or nineteen, didn't you ever think about what it would be like to have sex with someone, and there's this boy about your age right there in your house?"

"I'm not talking about this with my husband here."

"You don't have to. Just grant me that it could happen." Zigman pushed out a folder. "In here is a copy of a State Journal story that Ethel found."

Larson swept by with a bottle of Northleaf Liquid Happiness—sweet muscato sauvignon. She refilled Hall's glass.

Hall took a sip and set the glass aside. "I'm working on a research project for the library, about the Ku Klux Klan in southern Wisconsin, and I came on this story about a state investigation of the Klan in Nineteen Twenty-two. In that story, William J. Morgan, our state attorney general at that time, names the top one hundred Klan members in our southern counties."

Zigman sat back in his chair. He folded his hands across his stomach. "Want to guess who's on the list?"

He looked at Farquare.

The Cracker turned over a card showing a white whale flinging a boatload of sailors in the air with its tail. "Old Man Brinkmann."

"It's my guess," Zigman went on, "that Brinkmann was horrified when his nineteen-year-old daughter presented him with a black baby, a mixed-race baby. He couldn't have that and hold his head up in the

Klan. So he disposes of the baby and buries it in the garden, or he has one of his Klan friends do it. And he disowns his daughter. That's why she's not mentioned in the obits."

He tilted his head toward Stennard. "Remember what our medical examiner found when she examined the bones? A crack in the baby's skull."

Farquare peered up from the card showing Moby Dick's havoc. "What are you going to do now, give this to Denly the newspaper publisher? He and his wife started all this when they found the casket."

"And risk the trouble Akeema and I would be in with the sheriff? Denly would run with the story, you know that."

The Cracker combed his fingers back through his hair and ended with a brisk scalp rub. "Yeah, he would. I would, too, if I were still in the newspaper business."

Zigman came forward. He planted his elbows on the table, his hands clasped together. "For me, I'm going to do just what the sheriff would want me to do, put all these files in my bottom desk drawer and forget them. There's no proof of the cause of the child's death here or of who may have killed Baby Bee that a prosecutor could take to court. Everyone who was or may have been involved in this is dead, long, long dead."

Maredith Farquare looked like she had just touched an electric fence in which the juice was live. "That's it? What about the black family? The boy, the baby's father?"

"There's nothing in the records in the Wappello

Room that gives even a hint of what happened to the family. I know. I went back and looked."

"So all we have is a big zero?"

"Maybe not." Zigman waved his hands over the files and his notes. "I'm thinking that perhaps when I retire in twenty years or so, I just might give all this to the library, to the Wappello Room—it's a part of our history—so someone else can discover what we've discovered."

May

The Building of Bennettsville
by John

IT JUST SORT of emerged.

Real estate is cheap in Bennettsville, being one of the smallest towns in southern New Mexico. It's hot here all year round and even hotter in August.

No one ever comes here, and there is no such thing as a booming business. The boomingest is The Longhorn Saloon & Grill. We also have Leon's Grocery and Elton's Butcher Shop, the three businesses all right next to each other.

If it's excitement you want, you have to go two towns over–about an hour's drive. Here for excitement we watch the constable make his rounds, going from the school to Leon's, Elton's, The Longhorn, then turning left at the Catholic Church at the end of the street and heading back around to the school. We bet on whether today he'll change his route. So far, no one who's ever bet on change has won.

We do have some farms nearby. They grow chili peppers and beans, but that's about it.

That all changed when Thaddeus Thermopolis came to town, a developer from New Jersey. He rented a vacant store front and set up shop as Dreams Real Estate, slogan: "We turn dreams into real estate!"

Two days later, he bought some land.

Four days later, he begun construction on a new building.

Six days later, the building was taller than anything else in the town.

Two weeks after that, they'd pushed the building up to 200 stories. The steelworkers that high up looked like ants to those of us on the ground.

Thermopolis had money, and we learned he was not afraid to spend it . . . to, by God, build the world's tallest building.

When it topped 4,000 feet, it looked like it had passed the sky and grazed the moon. I swear, there's a brand new scratch on the moon's surface and I think this building caused it.

Our days are longer now because, as the old sun is setting in the west, it seems we can see the new sun reflecting high up on the building's east side.

I steeled myself and went into the building once, into the lobby, and the lobby seemed to be bigger than our town. This was the future, a lot of people in business suits texting on iPhones flitting by like gnats in the summer.

Us townsfolk, we're out of place. We all dress the same every day while the business men and women at The Thermopolis Tower have more suits than there are days in the month. I've never seen so many suits or smelled so many different colognes and perfumes at one time before. I thought I might die from exposure.

The top of the building is something else. It rises three stories every day. Says Thermopolis from his penthouse suite, "We're creating jobs."

And he is.

He's employed all the adults from 50 miles around and even made a deal with the school board that lets our high school students work at The Tower a half a day every day. Work/study they call it.

A terrible thing happened the day the building topped 5,000 feet. A high school kid on his first afternoon driving a crane rammed it into the side of the building. The building vibrated. It shook, and the upper stories began to topple, glass raining from the sky. Then the building dropped like a shot, collapsing, the weight of the mass driving a hole so deep into the ground that there was an earthquake.

No one survived other than me because I didn't work there.

Later that day, Thermopolis, who had been in Albuquerque visiting with the governor, drove back to Bennettsville.

He stepped out of his limo and surveyed the disaster, but the look on his face wasn't one of shock or even disappointment. He called his driver over and said, "We can turn this into something new and even better. Real estate is gonna be really cheap now."

Take My Hand
by Jerry

HATTY BROWN STUDIED the new guy, a gangly six-footer of indeterminate age, the fellow togged out in jeans, a sweater, and cowboy boots. Cowboy boots? In Wisconsin? She shook her head. "Have you ever done this before?" she asked.

As she had done, he shook his head. "No, I usually sub at the high school–shop and gym classes."

"Well, today you're a first grade teacher. I have Miss Carroll off at a curriculum meeting. She left her lesson plans for you. Follow those and you shouldn't have any trouble."

She waved for him to follow her down the hall, pointing out the boys and girls bathrooms on the way. "Never let a child go alone. Always send them in twos. That way you're pretty sure to get them back." She touched his arm, as if she were about to share a confidence. "They're used to going by twos. They'll call you on it if you don't work that way. What's your name again?"

"Mister Armstrong. Jack Armstrong."

"The all-American boy?"

He arched an eyebrow.

"It was an old radio show my dad listened to when he was a kid. I guess I'm giving away my age, aren't I?" She motioned to the room to their left, the room still dark. "Second grade there. Missus Tingley, she'll come dashing in just seconds before the moms start dropping off their children. Good teacher, even if she does worry me that some morning she's going to be late."

At the next door, she reached inside and flipped a switch, flooding the room with light from batteries of florescent tubes that buzzed like so many angry bees. "Your home for the day. Each child's name's on the front of his or her desk so you know who you have. Little kids, Mister Armstrong, you'll find they're like cows. They come to their assigned stalls every time."

He wandered in as she went back up the hall. He found a closet near the teacher's desk and parked his Packers slicker and cap there. He'd heard the forecast on TV over breakfast, rain before the end of the day. His book bag he dropped beside the desk.

Ahh, there they are, the lesson plans.

He scanned them, each block of time noted with what his students were to do, what they were to achieve according to standards some committee at the state department of education had established. What they were to achieve translates in non-academic talk, he knew, to what they were to learn. The standards were there in a binder at the side for reference, a big arrow drawn in red on the lesson plans, the arrow pointing at the binder.

The binder . . . this he stuffed in a bottom drawer and toured the room—a flock of desks, each too small for him to ever fit in; a Sponge Bob rug with a rocking chair, the reading area; a row of cubbies along the side wall; and a series of tables with art supplies laid out, drawing paper and boxes of crayons. He liked the red ones. He remembered chewing on them when he was a little kid, eating them, waxy with a taste so curious he could never describe it to anyone. He'd resort to holding a stub he had not yet devoured out to his mother and saying, "You try it."

Crayons . . . he opened a box and ran a finger over the dulled points. This was going to be a fun day.

He heard the shuffling of small feet coming through the classroom doorway. He wheeled around, summoning up his warmest smile. "Hi," he said.

Two urchins stood there, perplexed, confused, a Batman lunch box in the hand of one.

He figured they were thinking they must be in the wrong room. "Are you in Miss Carroll's class?" he asked.

Both nodded. In unison.

"I'm Miss Carroll today."

"No, yerrrr noooot," the boy with the lunch box said.

"You're right. I'm Mister Armstrong." He made a muscle with his right arm and pointed to it.

More perplexed looks.

The two, and the trio behind them, shambled over to their cubbies and shucked themselves of their belongings, then wandered on to their desks where they gabbled together as more students drifted in.

He went to the board and, in the upper right corner, printed in block letters the day of the week and, under it, he signed his name: *Mr. Arms* –

erased it and block printed MR. ARMSTRONG.

Someone tugged at his pant leg. He looked down at a blonde girl in glasses.

"I can't read that," she said.

He squatted down to her level. "That's me. That's my name." He held out his hand to her. "I'm Mister Armstrong, your teacher for today."

She shook his hand. "Mister Armstrong. I can remember that. I'm Ellie."

"Do you have a last name?"

"Uhmm, Tellwind." She smiled at her effort at memory paying off.

He saw that a front tooth was missing and motioned at the gap. "That happen recently?"

"Yesss, I got a dollar for it." She turned away and skipped back to her desk, announcing to her desk mates, "That's Mister Armstrong. He's our teacher today."

He dug a pile of books out of his book bag while a glut of children burst through the doorway, some stopping to stare at him, others unaware that there was a stranger in their room as they shot on to their cubbies.

He stacked the books on the corner of the desk, straightening the pile as the bell rang . . . or chimed over the P.A.

"All rise and face the flag," said a voice over the P.A., the voice belonging to Missus Brown. "I pledge allegiance . . ."

Hands went over hearts. His students shouted the pledge, like they were in a contest with the kids in the classroom across the hall, to see who could be the loudest.

"... with liberty and justice for all."

The kids settled and, after some moments, the squirming ceased.

Ellie raised her hand.

"Yes?"

"Mister Armstrong, are you gonna take roll? You have ta do that."

"I didn't know. You want to do that for me?"

She and the girl across from her in the next aisle burst from their desks and hustled to his desk where Ellie found the attendance card and the two marked who was there and who wasn't.

Done, Ellie looked at the class. "Who wants milk today?"

Hands shot up, and she and her partner counted them, agreeing after some discussion that fourteen wanted milk for the mid-morning milk break. She printed the number in the right place on the card, and the two carried the card out to the hall where they placed it in a kraft paper pocket taped beside the door.

"Any other chores we need to do?" he asked after Ellie and her partner returned, giggling about what he didn't know.

She shook her head.

"Well," he said, "I see from Miss Carroll's notes that we're to start with math."

HE GLANCED UP from his book, Levison Wood's *Walking the Himalayas*, when the herd came thundering down the hall, pounding in from recess, the kids laughing and gabbling. Somehow he had been excused from playground duty, so he had used the break to lose himself in a couple chapters about Levison's sojourns through Bhutan.

He swung his boots off the desk as Ellie and her friend came racing up. They leaned against the desk, breathing hard and twisting on their toes.

"Yes?" he asked.

Ellie bumped her partner. "You ask him."

Giggling, she bumped back. "No, you ask him."

Ellie sucked in a big breath. "Mister Armstrong, why do you wear cowboy boots?"

He came forward in his chair so they were nose to nose. "Because I'm a cowboy. I ride horses. I rode my favorite horse to school today."

Her eyes grew as large as headlights, and she gave a wide-mouthed grin to her partner, as if to say did you hear that? Ellie swivelled her face back to him. "Where is he? Can we see him?"

"She, and I don't think so."

"Why not?"

He got up and shambled over to a bank of windows that looked out across the playground to a woods beyond, oak trees with a few maples and pines sprinkled in, Ellie and her partner glued one to each of his sides.

"See there–" He motioned toward the tree line. "–just beyond that big red maple? Back there is where I tied Peg so she'd be in the shade and she'd be cool. Her real name is Pegasus."

Ellie pressed her nose against the glass. "I can't see her."

"Well, she's back under the trees."

She turned her face up to his. "What's she like?"

"Well, she's red, and she can fly."

"Really?"

"Like Buckbeak, the hippogriff in Harry Potter. Did you see the movie, The Prisoner of Azkaban?"

"Yeah." Ellie grabbed his hand and hauled him over to the art tables where everyone else had settled and were engrossed in drawing pictures with their crayons. "Hey, everybody, Mister Armstrong has a horse and she flies!"

The traveling art teacher, watching and listening from the doorway, came over to him. She whispered, "Now how're you gonna get yourself out of this one?"

He knew her from subbing a day at the middle school. He gazed up at the ceiling. "Sometimes I just get carried away with a good story."

"Don'tcha now." She moseyed away, to the classroom's smartboard, where she tapped the ON switch. "All right, children, today we're going to work on our colors and talk about which ones go best together for a particular effect."

HE LOOKED UP at the clock showing one minute before he was to dismiss his class to go to the lunchroom. He spun both hands over his hands. "All right, line up by twos. Get your lunch buddy."

All made it after some shoving and pushing except for one little guy with thick glasses, meandering around with a lost expression. Another boy, in line, this one with spiky hair, waved at the wanderer, calling to him, "Owen, come on you nit.

We got pizza today."

The minute hand touched the time and off they marched with Ellie holding his hand and her partner holding onto hers. "You gonna eat with the other teachers?" she asked.

He looked down at her. "No, I thought I'd eat with you."

"Really? Miss Carroll never does that."

"I guess she doesn't know what she's missing. Of course, you'll have to show me where everything is. I've never been here before."

That's all Ellie needed. She broke into a trot, dragging him into the cafetorium and to the beginning of the food line. She handed him a compartmentalized tray and announced with much pride to the cafeteria worker, "Our teacher's gonna eat with us."

The cafeteria worker snickered as she placed a slice of pepperoni pizza on his tray and a fistful of carrot sticks and a scoop of peach slices. "Good luck fitting in our tables. Be sure to get a squirt of ranch dressing for your carrots and a milk before you sit down."

He moved on to "the everything else" table and helped himself to a shot of dressing, a chocolate milk, a napkin, and a spork. A spork? That brought back memories.

Ellie bumped him. "Come on, Mister Armstrong, move it. You're holdin' up the line."

A spork, he looked at the all-purpose eating utensil again as he went along, falling in behind Ellie and her partner who scooted on to an open table.

This was a table with fixed bench seats, just right for little kids to get into, but . . . Oh, well. He set his tray down and worked one leg between the bench and the table. He sat and, by grabbing his knee with one hand and his ankle with the other, he maneuvered his outside leg inside the bench. Then he straightened his legs, pushing his feet forward until they came to rest under the bench seat opposite, okay until kids piled on that bench, at least two stepping on his ankles. He hauled his feet back and his knees bumped up under the table.

"How's yer pizza?" Ellie asked as she dipped a carrot stick in a blob of dressing on her tray.

"Looks good." He bit the point off his slice and chewed. "Hey, this is good."

"Yeah, we all like it, too. If you don't want your carrot sticks, I'll take some."

Another class rambled into the cafetorium, walking past his table. Ellie popped up and shouted to the new students, "Hey, this is our teacher! He's eating with us!"

HE FELT THE FLOOR vibrating and laid his book aside. Certain the herd was coming in from lunchtime recess, he pushed himself up and strolled to the door. There he greeted each arrival by name—names and faces, he was a quick study.

Ellie broke away from the others. She grabbed his hand and hauled him over to the windows, pointing toward the trees. "Mister Armstrong, your horse isn't there. Tam and I went out to look for her an' she's gone. She ran away, Mister Armstrong. How'll you get home?"

He rubbed at the hair on the back of his neck, puzzled by that one. "Well, I guess I'll have to walk."

She gazed up at him, sorrow in her eyes. "How far is it?"

"Five miles."

"My mom will give you a ride."

The traveling art teacher had followed the class in. After she collected some of her gear, she came over to him. "Digging yourself in deeper, huh?"

"Seems I'm really good at that. Hey, story time is next. You want to be our guest reader?"

"Sorry, I have to get back to the middle school."

He shrugged and went to his desk where he sorted down through his pile of books. He pulled out one, *The Adventures of Captain Underpants*, one of his favorites for reading aloud, and circled up everyone on the Sponge Bob rug. He settled in the rocking chair.

Ellie wagged her hand.

"Yes?"

"That's not the right book."

"But I like it, and you'll like it."

"Miss Carroll is reading us *The Magic School Bus*. We learned about 'lectricity and how plants grow. She said today we're supposed to learn about dinosaurs." She marched to the book cart and returned with a box set of Magic School Bus books. She took out one—*The Magic School Bus in the Time of the Dinosaurs* —and laid it in his lap. "You're supposed to start on the first page."

———

THREE-TEN, he made it. He parked his knuckles on his hips and looked out over his charges. "All right," he announced, "put everything in your desks except your assignment sheets and the books you're taking home for homework. They go in your backpacks, all right? And it's raining out there, so, if you've got a rain jacket and boots, put 'em on."

Desk lids came up and most shoved their stuff inside while a few took time to place each item in singlely—the neatniks of life, like his fiancé who drove him nuts with her orderliness.

Then came the scramble around the cubbies with those whose moms had sent them with rain gear getting dressed for the weather. Owen the wanderer sat on his butt on the floor, struggling with a rubber boot. He stooped to help, but Ellie stopped him.

"He can do it," she said.

"But he's putting the boot on the wrong foot."

"Miss Carroll says it's okay."

He sighed and went to the door where the first were waiting to leave. He gave each a touch on the shoulder or the back of the head along with a goodbye and their name as they passed before him and out into the hallway and freedom.

Ellie and her partner came up, each harnessed into her backpack and Ellie in her yellow slicker and yellow rain hat. "You gonna be our teacher tomorrow?" she asked, giving him her tooth-gapped smile.

"Only if Miss Carroll comes down with chicken

pox or breaks her leg. I don't think either of those things are going to happen."

"Maybe Tam and me can have her trip over Owen, then you could come back on Friday. We like you, Mister Armstrong."

"I like you, too. And you, too, Tam."

"How you gonna get home, Mister Armstrong?"

"I can probably get a ride with Missus Brown, don't you think?"

"But my mom—"

"I know."

"Okay, then." She trudged away with her partner beside her. But the trudging lasted only a few steps and she broke into a skip and then ran, hollering to someone ahead, "Wait for us."

Not a bad day. Not a bad day at all. He packed his books, pulled on his own slicker, and slung his book bag over his shoulder. Cap in hand, he strolled out into the hallway where he stopped at each classroom door to wave to a colleague-for-the-day and say thanks. At the office, he rapped on the door jamb.

Missus Brown glanced up from her paperwork, her look suggesting relief that her own day, too, was nearing an end. "Mister Armstrong, I've heard nothing but good things about you today. Will you come back if I call you?"

"Anytime."

"And about your horse—"

"She's not lost. She's in the parking lot."

He swung away and on outside into the drizzle that was tailing off, the sun poking through the first gaps in the clouds to the west.

As he neared the parking lot, he brought out his key fob and punched the doors-unlock button. Headlights ahead flashed on a red Mustang, its license plate reading PEG O1.

June

Broken Arrow
by John

DAY AFTER DAY, in the June heat at approximately 3:23 p.m., the engineer would climb up the twenty-five foot ladder to the top of the missile. A fifty-megaton gray masterpiece. It was decorated head to toe in yellow and black crisscross gravity stickers and warnings: "DANGER! PLUG IN ALL SAFETY VALVES WHEN NOT IN USE, CAUTION! DEADLY! NOT A TOY! IF NOT ALL OF THE SAFETY VALVES ARE PLUGGED IN, MELTDOWN WILL OCCUR!

Simple things like that catch the eye.

The engineer seemed more like a janitor in his line of work. He would climb the ladder and screw in any loose screws and swipe away any dusty spots on the top.

As the engineer passed them day in and day out, the big scary warnings felt more like motel paintings. The ladder climb itself became more and more every day, like something he could do in his sleep. His tedium tired eyes sunk even further by 3:20, knowing he had to clink his way up the ladder in three minutes.

The clock read 3:22, and something was off. The engineer had not finished his same boring turkey sandwich lunch yet or even gathered his things.

When he saw the clock, he shoved the last of the bread in his mouth, washed it down with cold coffee, and ran with his toolbox as fast as his stick legs would carry him.

3:24.

A minute late, but he was there. He took his first steps up the ladder as usual, climbing through the jungle of wires, trying to be careful not to unplug anything, although he could probably make this climb with his eyes closed. But as he got to the middle, he sighed. There was nothing less enjoyable than being suspended in the air uncomfortably for an hour, shining metal and tightening bolts.

He made his way through the last mass of wires and warnings. DO NOT CRACK, BREAK, UNPLUG, OR DAMAGE ANY WIRES. FRAGILE. The engineer yawned.

He reached the top and placed his toolbox on the top step of the ladder. The missile silo's roof was open today, the sun big and bright, high above the horizon. The engineer felt the warmth of the sun on his face and the warmth of the missile on his hand. He took an unusually long moment peering up at the sky. He kept his gaze fixed there, wanting more than anything to be away from the tediousness of his job. But a job's a job, and a cloud passed in front of the sun.

SHINING THE MISSILE took longer than usual, but he was finally done with it. He did, however, notice some loose screws.

He rolled his eyes and placed the polishing

equipment down hard on a platform beside the ladder. He kept his hand there a little longer. The sun then came out again. He looked up and enjoyed an unexpected feeling of optimism. He was almost done for the day, just a few screws to tighten and maybe a little bit more polish to put on on the way down and he was done.

He smiled a smile as large as the missile and gazed straight up into the sun, knowing that his mother had warned him never to do that, but he was not one to listen to warnings, and it was just too beautiful a day.

At last, he pinched his eyes shut, to shield them from the sun, and lost his balance. He grabbed the top of the ladder. Something, though, banged against the side of the missile—his toolbox falling, sheering through wires, ripping out a power strip as it plunged toward the bottom of the silo. The slight warmth the missile gave off turned into that of a microwave about to explode.

And the engineer enjoyed his sunshine.

Temptation
by Jerry

THREE YEARS INTO COLLEGE and I was entitled to a vacation. So I applied for a job as a park ranger at Yellowstone . . . and got it.

My first assignment?

Bear patrol.

Yellowstone's grislies are panhandlers. They sit at the side of the road and beg. And there's always some city fool who thinks, wow, wouldn't this make a great picture, me feeding a bear? So Mom holds the cell, ready to snap the shot, while Dad runs down the window and hands the bear a PB&J or a Snickers bar. Now you and I know the bear's going to take the sandwich and the hand. So my job was to sit up in the crow's nest close to the hottest begging area and bellow into a bullhorn: "Don't do that! Don't feed the bears! If you do and you live, you'll get a ticket and a five-hundred-dollar fine!"

Two weeks of doing that every day and all day long in the hot sun and your brain cooks. So another bear barker and I decided to have some fun on our day off.

You know Old Faithful? During the night, we pounded a post into the ground off to the side of the geyser, and we set a wagon wheel flat, balanced on top of the post.

The next morning about 11:00, with some 200 people gathered around to watch Old Faithful erupt, and, one minute to go, I stepped up to the wagon wheel and Bob walked out in front of the crowd, both of us in our park uniforms. Bob brought out his watch and started the countdown. Ten seconds before the geyser was to go off—we could feel the rumbling in the ground—he threw me a hand signal and I spun the wheel. To the guests, it looked like I was opening a valve, and up comes Old Faithful, blasting boiling water 106 feet into the air.

Everyone applauded us, and we took our bows . . . everybody applauded but our supervisor. He fired us, his sense of humor being no more than a rock's.

July

Base on Balls
by John

Pa loved July,
Often times more than me.
We, a poor, dusty family, and the crops
Don't grown no more.

Pa says he loves the dust.
Says it reminds him of bein' a kid.
As a kid, he had a diamond,
A diamond field made of dust.

Now Pa ain't no kid no more.
He's old and dyin.'
He's been layin' down and talkin'
Less and less.

Pa was a tough father.
Kept me on my toes and never
Went easy on me.
When I was bad, he'd hit me.
When we played, he'd hit me, too.

He taught me to throw a ball.
"Arm bent, throw from your legs," he'd say.
When I did it wrong, he'd hit me and show me again.
"Arm bent, throw from your legs."

"This dust has been real hard on us," Ma says.
Pa can't do nothing except remember and
He would say something every now and again.
"Where's my glove?" he'd say.

"Where's my glove?" he'd ask Ma.
Pa loved that glove, oft more than me.
He kept it with him all these years.
Ma said he was the best thrower in the county.

"He could strike out any batter," she'd say,
"Even Jesus." Then she'd cross herself
And say amen.
"He could hit, too. With a bat." Ma would begin to
cry.

I went in the room Pa was layin' down in.
"Hello, Pa," I said. He stared out the window.
"Pa, you was tough on me," I said.
"You a man. You's need to be tough," he said.

Pa stared out the window.
He was off somewhere on a field.
"Strike three," he said to himself and smiled.
Pa couldn't move much no more.

I didn't love Pa. He was tough.
He liked diamonds better than me and Ma.
He liked throwin' better than me.
He was good at throwin', but not love.

"Pa, I don't love you," I said to him, weak.
He began to cry. "Regret," he whispered.
"What's that, Pa? What do you regret?"
Pa looked at me and cried and said, "Base on balls."

The Man Left Behind
by Jerry

GLADYS MORTON LEANED from her chair far enough that she could see into James Early's office–Morton, the blue-haired secretary who believed she ran the sheriff's department. "Sheriff," she called out, holding her hand over her telephone receiver's mouthpiece.

Early, his feet up on his desk, folded down the copy of the Drover's Journal he had been reading. "Yeah, whatcha got?"

"Buck Thompson's on the line. He won't tell me why he's calling."

"And that bothers you?"

"Darn right. Says he'll only speak to you."

Early swung his feet down. He sprang from his chair to the door, closed it, then picked up the receiver from his desk telephone. "Buck?"

"Jimmy? You alone where no one can hear us?"

"Just a minute." Early pressed his receiver's mouthpiece to his chest and hollered toward the door, "Gladys? Hang up."

He put his receiver back to his ear and heard a click on the line. "All right, Buck, it's just you and me."

"Jimmy, Ernie Guest is dead. You need to get out here."

Early snatched a pencil from the Campbell's

Soup cup in which he kept his collection of writing utensils and hunched over his desk pad, ready to write. "Where's here?"

"The bluff behind Liloam School. And you come alone."

EARLY TURNED OFF the county road onto the lane that led to the Liloam School and beyond, Liloam the country school where Buck Thompson had taught all eight grades when he came home from the war. Since, he had gone back to K-State for graduate work and had stepped up to teaching science classes at Leonardville High School.

Doc Grafton, in the shotgun seat of Early's Jeep, squinted at the schoolhouse, its paint blistered and peeling, as they motored by. "He's not going to like it that you brought me along."

"Well, it's a death. Kansas law says you have to do your job and determine and report the cause."

"Yeah, maybe. My wife's on me to give it up."

"Doc, you'd get bored just being a doctor. You like a mystery." Early pulled off at the base of a bluff and eased his Jeep in between a county road grader and a Studebaker sedan he knew Thompson drove. He stepped out onto the dirt turned to dust by weeks of a blistering sun and looked up. Early gave a quick wave to a man above him, at the top of the bluff, the sky beyond cloudless and the merciless sun baking the day.

The man waved back but stopped when Grafton eased his bulk out of the passenger seat. "I thought I told you to come alone."

"Sorry, Buck, the law says the coroner has to be here."

"If he comes up, I'll throw him over the edge."

Early shrugged and thumbed Grafton back in the Jeep. He then hiked around to a trail and made the climb to the top. There before him sat Thompson on a rock, at his feet a blanket that covered something Early assumed was a body. "Ernie?" he asked as he mopped the sweat from his forehead with his sleeve.

Thompson made a half-hearted gesture toward the blanket.

Early came closer. He knelt on one knee and lifted the blanket back, revealing the head and torso, the torso in a tee-shirt, the tee-shirt green and faded from too many washings. The way the upper part of the body laid, with the head turned to the side, Early could see it, a portion of the back of the skull gone—blasted away. He peeled the blanket back some more until he could see one of the man's hands, in it a pistol. Early took note of the service insignia on the grip—Marines—the pistol a standard issue Colt Forty-Five, this one a war souvenir. Early, too, had kept the Forty-Five he'd lifted from a dead officer when he mustered out of the Army. He looked up at Thompson, Thompson's eyes red, his hair disheveled. "What do you think, he ate his gun?"

"Jimmy, I never saw it coming. Ernie was such a quiet guy. You met him at the Grange hall last year. He was one of my election judges."

Early pushed himself up. He took his time slapping the dust out of the knee of his tan trousers. "I remember him."

"He drives–drove–drove that grader down there for the county. He was a Marine in the South Pacific, did you know that?"

"You told me."

"Everyone in his platoon, Jimmy, they were all killed at Iwo. He was the only survivor, and he felt terrible about it. Guilt, you know. When the memories would get too much for him, he'd come up here and draw, scenics, never any people. Ernie got to be real good over the years." Thompson held up an artist's pad. "I found this over by the edge of the bluff, a stone on it and a note under the stone saying he wanted Eldora Wilson to have it. She was one of my election judges, too."

"I remember her."

Thompson rubbed at his leg where his artificial limb fit up around his stump. "Climbing up here twice raised hell with my stump. Man, it hurts."

"Twice?" Early asked.

"I had to go down to get to a phone to call you, then climb back up here with the blanket from the trunk of my car, from my winter survival kit."

"It's nearly July."

"I keep it in my car year round." He straightened the fabric of his trouser leg before he stood up. "Jimmy, you can't call this suicide."

Early swept his hand over the body. "Everything here points to it–"

"You don't understand."

"Apparently not."

"Ernie's memory with his friends doesn't need suicide hung on it. The talk it'd create, and he'd be denied military rites."

Early moved away to think. He paced. After some moments, he went over to the edge of the bluff and called down to Grafton, "Doc? Come on up."

Grafton waved, and Early went back to Thompson paging through Guest's art pad. "How'd you know Ernie was up here?"

Thompson closed the cover on the pad and used it to fan himself. "When I drive by, I always look to see if the road grader's here or Ernie's pickup. If one is, I stop and come up and we talk for a while. This morning it was the grader."

"He have any family I should notify?"

"Not really."

"Meaning?"

"Ernie's parents, they died some years back."

"Brothers? Sisters?"

"He did have one sister."

"Where's she?"

"Don't know. She moved away during the war and Ernie lost contact with her. By now, she could be married with six kids or be dead herself."

"A wife?"

Thompson shook his head. "Never married. So for a family, about the closest he had was Eldora and I guess me."

Grafton topped the bluff and huffed his way over, fanning himself with his hat. "That's one helluva climb," he said. "So what have we got here?"

When neither Early nor Thompson answered— both stood looking off at the horizon, in the direction of Fort Riley, the big Army reservation less than a dozen miles away–Grafton went over to the body. He gazed down at it, the top half exposed to the world. "Good Lord, he blew his brains out."

Early sighted a red-tailed hawk circling, drifting toward the bluff. Had to be a red tail from its blunt profile. "Is that what you're gonna put in your report?"

"Suicide? The evidence is right here." Grafton gestured at the pistol.

Early turned around, his hands in his back pockets, sadness creasing his face. "Doc, Ernie, Buck, me and you, we were all in the war. The only ones who got any peace out of it were the dead. Those who came home, a lot came home damaged. Ernie was one, maybe you didn't know that. Doc, he doesn't deserve to be branded with suicide, so call it something else."

"But people will know."

"Only the three of us. Well, four. Brownie at the mortuary 'cause he gonna get the body. He won't tell and neither will we."

"But the funeral–"

"Closed casket."

Grafton sighed. "Well, I suppose I could put down heart attack. That's what kills most people who don't die of old age, so nobody'll question it."

Early massaged Grafton's shoulder. "Thanks." He motioned to Thompson, waved for him to join him at the body. Together they lifted the blanket away and laid it on the dust.

The smell released by the air hitting the soaked trousers of the dead man–Early winced. "We sure do mess our britches when we die, don't we?"

Thompson sat back on his heels. "We could strip off his pants—"

"No, this has been degrading enough for him. He doesn't need to be half naked. You take his shoulders now. I've got his ankles. On three, we lift him onto the blanket."

Early made the count, and, on three, he and Thompson hefted the body over to the blanket and wrapped it.

Early came up in a crouch. He worked his hands under the body and lifted, hoisted it up and across his shoulder. "I'll tote him down," he said as he straightened up under his burden. "We'll put him in the back of my Jeep."

EARLY DOODLED on the pad on his desk, his telephone's handset pinched between his shoulder and the side of his head. "That's it? You're not gonna give us a caisson?"

A man's voice came back over the handset, a rumbling baritone. "Can't do it, Jimmy. He wasn't Army."

"Punch, you're gonna quibble about that?"

"I don't make the rules. I tell you what, I can detail an honor guard to be there."

"Forget it. I'll get some Marine vets to do the job." Early hung up. He wanted to slam the handset into its cradle, but what good would that do? It'd still only be a click on the line.

Thompson, cleaning his fingernails with his pen knife, stared at Early. "No luck with the adjutant?"

Early shook his head.

"I didn't have high hopes, but the casket on a caisson and a four-horse team pulling it to the cemetery, that would have been something."

Early started a new doodle that took the shape of a Jeep. He continued it, adding a casket riding on the back and a flag draped over the casket. Early turned his doodle to Thompson. "How about this? A lot of the dead were brought off of battlefields on Jeeps."

RED VOLMER, microphone in hand, elbowed his way through the crowd on the sidewalk to the curbing. He glanced back and up to the window of K-MAN'S second-floor studio and shot his pointer finger at his engineer.

"This is Red Volmer," he said into his microphone, turning back to the street. "I'm here at curbside to bring you all the details of Manhattan's Fourth of July parade in this, our station's first live broadcast of this event."

He held his microphone, the cord wrapped around his arm, above the heads of those around him and aimed it down the street, shouting up at his microphone, "You hear it now, the muffled drums? That's the beginning of the parade. The first unit is moving this way."

Volmer brought his microphone down, and, as he did, he stepped out into the street for a better view. "It's a color guard," he said to his microphone. "People jamming the sidewalks, as the flag gets closer, they're taking off their hats and caps and putting their hands over their hearts. Some are saluting. I can see them now. The color guard is made up of Marine Corps veterans from the Second World War. Hard to believe that war ended only eight years ago, isn't it, and we're now in a war in Korea.

"Behind the color guard, I can see, is a drum corps. They're from the Pearce-Keller American Legion Post, I know that. Behind them, oh, it's a Jeep. And there are more legionnaires. They're marching on either side of the Jeep. I'm going to get closer to see if I can get you the story here."

Volmer retreated, and the color guard and the drum corps passed by. After they did, he saw a break between the marchers who followed and shot through them to the Jeep. There he jammed his microphone in the face of the driver, James Early, Early in his Army dress uniform, a single chevron on the sleeve. "Sheriff, can you stop a sec?"

"No, but how about I slow down?"

"All right. Tell us about this. I see you've got what looks like a casket on the back of your Jeep, and that's an American flag's draped over it, right?"

Early motioned for his partner in the passenger seat—Buck Thompson, also in Army Class A's—to take the question.

Thompson leaned into the microphone. "Ernie Guest died a couple days ago. He was a World War Two vet, a Marine in the South Pacific—Iwo Jima. You know the picture of the men raising the flag on Mount Suribachi? The company Ernie fought with made that possible, so we in the Legion post thought this was a good way to honor him. We're gonna end up at the cemetery after the parade. Maybe you'll want to be there."

Volmer, at the end of his microphone cord, pulled away, not sure what he should say as the Jeep drove on, the honor guard keeping in step with it. The sound of a band blaring out *Semper Fidelis*, the Marine Corps march, caused him to turn. "It's the high school band," he said as he stepped back to the curb.

THE LEGION POST'S rifle squad triggered off their volley, the sound fading away among the trees that softened all sounds at the Sunset Cemetery. Two members of the honor guard, wearing white gloves, took that as their cue to lift the flag from the casket and begin the slow, measured ceremony of folding the flag. Early and Thompson watched. When the guardsmen finished, one presented the flag to Thompson.

Thompson choked. After some moments, he stammered to the guardsman, "This, uhm, this flag . . . ah, this flag will fly in front of the Grange hall where—you know, I didn't think this would be so hard for me, but it is." He sniffled and passed the flag to Early.

Early, surprised, glanced at Thompson tearing up. He looked to the guardsman. "What Buck wants to say is that Ernie Guest served on his team of election judges. Their polling place was the Cottonwood Grange hall. He's sure Ernie would be proud that this flag will be there."

The guardsman stepped back one pace. He gave a slow, deliberate salute to Thompson and to Early, did an about face and, with his partner, marched away.

The graveside service concluded, others drifted off, most of them war vets, Early knew, most in uniforms that still fit, some in battle fatigues, a few from World War One in their Sunday suits and Legionnaire overseas caps.

He and Thompson lingered. They watched a cemetery crew fill in the grave at the head of which was rooted a white cross with Guest's name, dates, and service details carved into it, a white cross like those in the line to their right, most of them placed there as memorials to Riley County husbands, fathers, and sons killed overseas.

Early slipped the flag back to Thompson.

Thompson held it to his chest and gazed at the now closed grave, the soil mounded up, the cemetery crew walking away. "This is a good thing we've done, don'tcha think, Cactus?"

"Yeah. Just wish we could have gotten a caisson."

"Really I think the Jeep was better."

"Yeah, it did work."

With the toe of his shoe, Thompson pushed a crumble of dirt up onto the side of the mound over the grave. "Well, Ernie's no longer the man left behind. He's with his buddies, his platoon mates killed in that damn war that killed so many. Will we ever be able to forget it?"

Early put his arm around Thompson's shoulders. "Not likely, Buck. No, not likely."

August

A Woman's Place
by John

DEBORAH LEE CAME through the back door carrying a grocery bag filled to the brim. She always cooked on Sundays and shopped just after church at the local market. She wore her finest yet shortest sun dress that allowed the sun to come through where it doesn't normally shine. The skirt had ridden up to an uncomfortable level in the car, so she snatched the hem down . . . and dropped the bag. Out spilled oranges and bananas and salad fixings.

She swore, then sighed in frustration and went about picking dinner up from the floor.

Deborah Lee was married, but her wedding ring got more of a workout than her husband Bill. He was a fat man who snored through Sunday sermons and gulped down the communion wine to relieve the headache from the night before. After church, he went to Sneakers and watched the Cowboys game with his oldest and best friends, Jack Daniels and Sam Adams.

These Sunday afternoons became Deborah's favorite times. She could cook and clean and shower and be the best housewife she could be. And she was a great housewife.

She loved her husband, more or less. She always cleaned for him and cooked for him. She would talk to him, but he was often too drunk or annoyed to answer back, so she let it slide.

She was a good housewife. Always listened to her husband and let him soften himself when he needed it.

She was a good housewife.

But this Sunday in particular, she really needed it. She had put in a hard week cooking and cleaning and ushering at church. She went to the fridge and pulled out a plate of cookies. The Saran wrap had been ripped and only two cookies and a few crumbs remained of the dozen and a half she had baked just yesterday. Exhausted and angry, she waltzed into the living room where she was greeted by someone in her husband's recliner.

"Bill?" Deborah asked.

But it wasn't.

The figure was too tall and muscular to be him.

She blushed and pushed a stray stand of hair behind her ear. "Well, well, well, Charlie," she said. "I've got two cookies left if you want one. I'm so glad to see you."

The figure said nothing, just sat there and stared out the window.

"I'll get us some milk," she said as she glided away to the kitchen. Deborah filled two glasses and closed the fridge, and there was the figure, seven feet tall with a lengthy beard and what seemed like sun-crisped skin.

It wasn't Charlie or Bill. Charlie, she knew, didn't have horns coming from his head.

"Oh my, you frightened me," she said with an

uncomfortable laugh. "I just wasn't expecting any company today. So, you're not from around here, right? Where are you from?"

She eased back toward the sink.

"Down south," the figure said.

Deborah forced a smile. "Dixon County?"

The figure didn't answer.

She continued to smile but cut off eye contact and turned away, to collect herself. When Deborah turned back, the figure was gone.

She swivelled towards the kitchen table, and there he was, in a chair. She gasped and then laughed at herself. "My, oh my, you sure are quick. And quiet. Would...would you like something to eat? I've made deviled eggs."

The figure stared at her.

Deborah, holding her smile, slipped over to the fridge where her deviled eggs were. "I've also got a pork roast left over. I'll put it in the microwave to heat."

She did just that, her hands shaking, shaking even when she unwrapped her tray of deviled eggs. "Sorry about calling you Bill earlier. He's my husband. And sorry I thought you were Charlie. He's a neighbor and good man, too."

Deborah wanted desperately to know who this man was who was in her house. She stared at him and saw that his skin was tough and cracked. That and his demeanor frightened her.

"So, umm, Bill is my husband, and I treat him well," she said with a nervous laugh, trying to make conversation. "I try to be hospitable and loving, but he makes it so hard. I'm a good wife. I cook, clean, and press his trousers and shirts when he needs them ironed. He can be a little stubborn, and I don't think I handle that well. He's also not very good down there—" She motioned to below her belt. "—but he's got money, and that's what I love about him. There is no absence of love, just a long hiatus."

She realized she was rattling on, confessing, as it were, for no good reason.

The figure just listened, never moving a muscle.

"And Charlie," Deborah continued, "the other man I thought you were, he's just a fine man. Kind, tender, and talented in all the right places. I mean, he's a good pastor and loves people. I just think the world of him. Bill was out of town the other night, so I made Charlie a roast. The dinner was all in good fun. Ain't nothing wrong with that."

The microwave dinged.

Deborah screeched at the sound.

"Oh my," she said, adding an innocent little laugh after she regained her composure, "I still scream whenever that thing goes off. Isn't that the silliest?"

She got up and opened the microwave, and steam rolled out the door. She pulled out the plate and set it on the counter. That's when she felt a tingle run down her spine. The figure had placed his hands on her shoulders.

Deborah began to cry. "The roast is ready," she said, snuffling, her shoulders shaking. "It may be a little hot, the plate. Here."

She turned and handed the roast to the figure. "I hope it's not too hot."

The Forever Deputy
by Jerry

*Note: Names, to me, are extremely important. Example: The deputy in this story originally was Lawton Moses. Now I have a Constable Mose Dickerson in other James Early stories, so I changed Lawton Moses to Lawton Dent, then Goode, and finally to Wells, trying to get the right sound for the last name. Yes, I know the movie, *The Outlaw Josey Wales*. Wales/Wells, the names are so close, still, despite what Clint Eastwood might desire had he known, I decided to stick with Wells.

LAWTON WELLS PLODDED in from the cornfield, a hoe over his shoulder, his face and arms slick with sweat—shot for the day—intent on reaching the stock tank, Nirvana for a tired farmer, only to see his wife racing away from the house, calling to him, her hair in a kerchief, her hands dusted with flour from breadmaking.

"What's got your dander up, old woman?" he hollered back.

"It's Jimmy Early. Says he needs you."

"He can wait." Wells dropped his hoe. He tossed his straw hat to the side, steadied his calloused hands on the water tank's rim, the steel cooling to the touch, then plunged his gray thatch under. Wells shook his head, stirring the tank full of nature's juice, and pulled up, reveling in the cold wet that washed off his head and down his chest and back. "Hoo-yah."

"Maybe you ought to jump in there, old man."

"He on the phone?"

"Yes."

"Cactus does have a habit of calling at the worstest of times." Wells stripped the water from his hair and face. "Nothing I'd like better than to pull off these bibs and swim. Hotter'n the hinges of Hades out in the field. What's our dear sheriff want?"

Jodie Wells recovered her husband's hat. She held it before her, biding her time. "Said there's a shooting."

"Wouldn't you know."

"Said he wants you there. I told him you're getting too old for this."

"Yup, well, Jimmy helped us with a job when we needed money." Wells dipped his hands in the water and splashed the wetness up over his biceps. "So as long as I can get around, I owe him to help. Hon, how about you get the truck out while I get the particulars?"

Wells took his hat and trotted off toward the house while Jodie hustled in the other direction, toward the corn crib, the drive-through a doorless garage for their pickup. The truck, old as it was, was a fooler. Wells and Early had dropped a Ford V-Eight under the hood several years back, and Early had tuned the big-bore engine so the truck would run like a Packard—ninety on the flats—an aid to Wells in his occasional work as a reserve deputy for the Riley County Sheriff's Department.

Dangerous work.

He lost his trigger finger in a shootout with a lone robber who had taken it on himself to stick up the Leonardville State Bank when Wells was down the street at the hardware store.

He clattered into the kitchen and grabbed up the receiver swinging from its cord. Wells put the receiver to his ear.

"What you got, Cactus?" he said into the mouthpiece of the wall phone.

"You know the little house where Simmie Frye and her boyfriend are living?" came James Early's voice back.

"Yeah."

"Gunfire between the house and somebody on the road. A neighbor called it in. I've got deputies way far away from there, and you know twenty minutes is the quickest I can get up there."

"So you want me to go over and arrest the yahoos."

"I wouldn't ask if I had somebody closer."

"You'll be glad to know I've already got Jodie's bringing the truck around." Wells pulled a yellowed sheet of telephone numbers from behind the phone, his eyes scanning for one. "I'll call Wink for backup."

"He's away at a funeral. You're the only one out there who's got a badge."

"Well, all right then. I'll try not to get myself killed."

"See you in twenty."

Wells placed the receiver up on the phone's hook. He stuffed the telephone numbers back where they were, then went to Jodie's broom closet. There he took down his Colt Forty-Five and a full magazine. He slammed the magazine into the pistol's grip and stuffed the gun in his back pocket. Next he took down two more magazines, a box of twelve-gauge shells, and his Remington pump and headed out the door toward where his wife waited with the truck idling.

"You drive," he said as he climbed into the passenger seat. "I've got a bad feeling about this one."

"Why's that?"

"There's shooting at Simmie Frye's house."

"Oh Lordy."

WORRY CLOUDED Jodie Wells' face as she herded the truck out into the lane, this woman with an industrial-strength build, a life-long country school teacher until she had given it up six years ago. At the end of the lane, she guided the truck onto the creek road and shifted up through the gears, getting up to forty-five on the rough gravel. She swung wide around a washboardy section.

Wells rode in silence, pushing shell after shell into his shotgun's magazine.

Jodie slowed for the turn onto County Twenty-Three. "Wink gonna meet you?"

"Cactus says he's at a funeral. I'm on my own for the time."

"Know any details?"

"Just gunfire between the house and the road."

"I never liked that boy Simmie's been living with."

The truck bounced through a rut, throwing Wells up toward the roof. Jodie clung tight to the wheel.

When Wells came down, he straightened himself around, glancing at his wife. "What makes you think it isn't Simmie with the gun?"

"Speed and Elvie's girl? You've known her since she was a baby, and I taught her in school." Jodie jerked the truck around a groundhog that had ventured into the road. The fat, built-low creature wheeled and scrambled back into the weeds of the borrow ditch.

Wells, a bandana in hand, polished the barrel of his shotgun. "Simmie's something of a wild hair."

"More like a free spirit."

"Maybe. Stop up here on the rise, wouldja? I'll take me a look."

Jodie took her foot from the gas pedal to the brake. She stepped down.

Wells reached under the seat as the truck rolled to a stop. He came out with a leather case. From it, he extracted his ten-power field glasses. Wells peered through them and fiddled with the focus knob. "Jesus H. Christ."

"What is it?"

"Speed's truck, down there in the road. Got to be him crouched behind it."

Four pops, in rapid succession, came up through the dusty, sticky heat of the half-mile distance.

"They sure aren't done peckin' at each other." Wells swung out of the cab. He closed the door and stepped back up on the running board, shotgun at his side. "Jo, you drive like hell down there. Slow a bit when you come up on Speed so I can jump, then get outta here. Get on into Leonardville, to Elvie's."

She tromped down on the accelerator, the rear tires spraying gravel as the truck raced away. At the last moment, as she neared Speed Frye's truck, Jodie downshifted. She touched the brakes, but too hard and flung Wells from the running board. He came down in the ditch, rolling, flattening a patch of horse nettle as she sped away.

Wells came up on his knees. He spit dirt as he checked himself for broken bones. Satisfied, he went after his shotgun and his hat, and scurried off, keeping low, back toward Speed Frye's truck, Frye leaning across the hood, sighting along the barrel of his Thirty-Ought-Six.

Wells scrambled out of the ditch and hunkered down by Frye's pant leg. "What the hell's goin' on?"

"What the hell ya think?" Frye kept his squint down the gun's sight.

"Jimmy called."

A gunshot came from the house.

Frye jerked the trigger. His rifle barked, and he yanked the bolt back, sending a spent shell flying to the side. "I'm a mite busy tryin' to keep myself from bein' killed."

"Why're you here anyway?"

Fyre rammed the bolt forward. He locked it down, a live round in the breech. "You know Boots

Teagen?"

"The boy your girl's living with?"

"Boy?! Mean summabitch. He went to beating on Simmie. She called me at the post office, hysterical. So I come out and returned the favor."

"Don't tell me you did."

"Damn right. Beat hell out of him, told him if he ever touched Simmie again, I'd kill him. Left him cowering behind the shithouse."

"So what's the shooting?"

"Summabitch got to his blaster just as I drove out. Shot out two of my tires."

"Oh, and you just happened to have that old Springfield and a pocket full of shells in your truck."

"You know I always have my rifle in a case behind the seat." Frye, more than a head shorter than Lawton Wells when the two stood side by side, glanced down. "Where's your shirt?"

"Left it in the field where I was chopping velvet weed. I'm gonna have some kinda rash, you know, where I came up in that horse nettle."

"Don't blame me. I didn't ask you out here."

A shot from the house blew the truck's hood ornament away. Frye sent a bullet back.

"So what're you gonna do?" Frye asked as he jacked the spent shell out of his rifle's firing chamber.

"Well, I know you aren't gonna shoot me, so I guess I'll go get Boots before his aim improves and he wings us both."

"How're you gonna do that? You go in from here, he'll cut you down."

"Jodie'd sure cuss me out if I let that happen."

Wells leaned around Frye. He studied the ditch in the direction from which he and Jodie had come. "What say I go in the back door."

"Uh-huh."

"I could scoot down the ditch to that draw below the house, cut across the road there. He won't see me for the trees."

"He's gonna hear you coming through the door."

"Speed, you sure can rain on a party."

"I don't want you gettin' shot unless I'm in your will to get Falstaff and Hotspur."

"My horses? Friend, that's sure not gonna happen. Tell you what, I'll throw my bandana above the roof. When you see it, you put a bullet through the window–high, mind you. While Boots is busy shootin' back at you, I'll go in." Wells pulled a spectacles case from his bib pocket. He opened the case and removed a pair of wire rims, hooking the bows over his ears.

"What are those for?"

"Neighbor, I got the eyes of an eagle from a distance. Close up, I need a little help. How many shells you got left?"

Frye glanced in the box open on the fender of his truck. "A dozen maybe."

"Good. Every ten seconds I'm in that house, you throw a bullet through that window. Keep him nervous."

Wells slapped the back of Frye's leg. Crouching low, he trotted off down the borrow ditch until a cluster of Osage orange trees and a ravine masked him from the house. Wells heard another exchange of gunshots as he crossed the road and plunged into a woods that carried around behind the backyard and garden that went with the one-story bungalow.

Brambles snagged at Wells' britches as he clambered over the first of two fallen trees. At the second, a dry rattle stopped him.

Wells scanned to one side, then the other. To the left, he spotted a vibrating motion. Below it a snake laid coiled, camouflaged in the leaves near the upturned roots of a cottonwood.

Wells eased back. He swung wide around the tree and some skunk cabbage, then scrambled up the side of the ravine to the flat. There he worked his way through a cluster of red haws that separated him from the garden and the raggedy backyard. At the side of the garden, Wells scooped up two green tomatoes, each the size of a baseball. He tied one in his bandana. The other he slipped in his pocket.

He again trotted on, this time to the back porch. There Wells stepped out of his shoes. He set them aside and flung his tomato-weighted bandana up for all he was worth. On the crack of a rifle shot, Wells eased open the screen door. A blur of fur flew past him, Simmie's mongrel dog racing away.

On the second shot, Wells with his shotgun slipped inside. He kept a hand on the doorjamb so the screen wouldn't bang shut. It banged instead on his fingers.

Wells grimaced. He pulled his fingers out of the door and shook the pain from them while he crept around the table to a short hallway. There he knelt. Wells took out the second tomato. He flipped it ahead, far ahead, the tomato bouncing and rolling along the plank floor.

"What the—" came a voice from the room at the end of the hall.

"You aren't the only one here, Boots."

"Wells? That you?"

"Yup. Seems you got yourself in a pickle, son."

"I'll kill you, old man."

"Oh, I don't think so. Speed and I kinda gotcha penned in."

"The hell you say."

"Boots, if you're dumb enough to go out the front window or the side, Speed's gonna cut you down. And if you're really dumb and try for the back door, well, you've gotta get past me, and I've got a scatter gun. Sure as God made that green tomato, I'll air you out." Wells hunkered himself down, laid flat on his belly, aiming his shotgun ahead. "There'll be nothing for the coroner to pick up but bits of meat and bone."

Wells reached for his back pocket and his pistol. He got it around in front of him, left his shotgun and wriggled along the base of the wall.

"Don't shoot my Boots."

What? A girl's voice?

Wells stopped. "Simmie?"

"Yes."

"Why in the name of heaven didn't you run, girl?"

"He didn't mean to hurt me, Mister Wells."

"That's for the judge to decide. Simmie, wherever you are, you keep out of the way. . . . Boots? You hear me?

"Yeah?"

"Throw your rifle out the window."

"Hell I will. Simmie, get over here!"

"No."

"Do it or I'll kill ya where ya are!"

A bullet ripped through the window. The girl screamed, and Wells rolled out. He glanced around the corner and as quickly rolled back—Boots Teagen in T-shirt and jeans to the side of the window, a deer rifle in his right hand and a nickel-plated revolver in his left, his left arm clutching Simmie Frye to his chest.

"Wells, I got Simmie as a shield. I'm coming out!"

"Aw, Bootsie boy, you don't want to do that. You cross in front of that window, Speed's gonna pick you off sure."

"Not if I've got his girl."

"He don't know that."

"Frye," Boots shouted.

"Yeah?" came a voice from the roadway.

"I got Simmie! Don't you shoot!"

Wells rolled right for another look. His eyes widened when he saw Teagan's revolver aimed at him. He kicked back. A blast, and his scalp burned.

A rifle shot from the road answered, splintering wood.

Wells kicked himself back into the doorway and jerked off two shots.

Teagan blanched. His revolver and revolver hand came around to his shoulder.

Wells, still on his belly, kept his pistol trained on Teagan. "Boots? Next one's in your head. Your brains and blood's gonna be all over Simmie. You want that? Drop your guns, boy. Let her walk away."

Teagan's rifle clattered on the floor, then his revolver. He fell back against the wall and slid down, blood streaking the dingy wallpaper behind him.

"What's goin' on in there?" came Speed Frye's voice from the roadway.

"I got him! It's over." Wells pushed himself up, his pistol still on Teagan. "Speed, leave your damn rifle out there!"

Simmie, on her knees with Teagan, cradled the wounded man. "You shot him, Mister Wells."

"Kinda had to." He pushed his free hand up to the top of his head and played his fingers over his scalp. They came away red. "Damn fool tried to kill me."

He kicked Teagan's revolver and rifle across the room, then knelt. Wells examined the man's wound. He kneaded at the flesh of Teagan's shoulder, Teagan wincing. "I tell you, boy, you're one lucky bunny. If I'd hit the bone, the doc would be lopping your arm off. Simmie, you got a towel?"

"In the kitchen."

SPEED FRYE BURST THROUGH the front door as Wells went out, down the hallway. "Simmie, Simmie, Simmie!" he called out as he made the turn. Frye tore his daughter away from Teagan.

She swung hard at her father's face.

Frye caught her hand. He spun her around and wrapped her in his arms. He hugged her, but she still sank her fingernails into his flesh.

Frye yelped and flung his daughter away.

Wells ambled back into the room, a couple towels in one hand and an extra that he held clutched in a wad on top of his head. "Now, now, children, bad enough I had to shoot Bootsie-boy. I don't want to have to shoot the two of you."

"You all right?" Frye asked.

"Jodie's gonna have to do a bit of needlework on my scalp. Speed, get the guns, and get my shotgun from the hallway. I'm gonna see if I can stanch this man's bleeding."

Wells again knelt beside Teagan. He wrapped a towel around Teagan's shoulder, drew the ends under the man's armpit and back up. "Simmie, make yourself useful. Get over here."

He took her hand and placed it on the makeshift bandage. "You hold that tight while I tie this flour sack around it."

The Martha White seal and printing had not fully bleached out of the cloth that Wells wrapped over the bandage. He thumbed his glasses up on the bridge of his nose, the better to see what he was doing as he worked the ends of the sack together in the first half of a square knot. He pulled down hard, and Simmie yanked her fingers away.

"No, no, you keep your fingers there." Wells nodded at the knot. "I don't want this to slip loose and him bleed to death before we get him to a doctor."

Again he knitted the ends of the flour sack together, and again he pulled the knot tight, Teagan groaning at the new pain.

"Oh, be quiet, knothead."

A siren broke through the musty gloom of the room, the siren's volume increasing.

"Speed, that's gotta be Cactus. Go out and wave him in while Simmie and I get this fool on his feet."

Frye, armed like a Confederate raider, dashed out of the house.

Wells got a hand under Teagan's good arm and, with Simmie's help, hauled him up. He worked his shoulder under Teagan's arm and guided the slumping man toward the door, Simmie hurrying ahead, her thin dress blood-spattered, her face twisted with concern.

They came out as a Jeep swung into the dirt drive. The Jeep bounced across and onto what little grass there was in the front yard, the siren winding down. Out stepped James Early, cattleman's hat at an angle, his ragged mustache showing some salt among the pepper. "Looks like I hurried for nothing," he said.

Wells nodded. The wadded towel slipped from his head, and he grabbed for it.

"Law, you all right?"

"Oh yeah. Old Bootsie wasn't quite quick enough to put me singing with the angels."

Early, as he strolled toward his reserve deputy and Wells' prisoner, glanced down at his deputy's stockings. "He shoot your shoes off?"

"Naw, left them on the back porch."

"Why'd you do that?"

"Long story."

"You know you've got a hole in the toe of one sock?"

Wells peered down. He wiggled the big toe peeking through. "Thought it felt a bit airy."

Early got his hand on the back of Teagan's belt. To Wells he said, "Shall we get him in the Jeep?"

"It's that or we make him walk to jail."

They shuffled off the porch and down into the yard.

"How bad's his wound?" Early asked.

"Tore hell out of his shoulder. A Forty-Five will do that. You may want to get somebody to patch him up."

"Can do."

The two horsed Teagan into the passenger seat where Early handcuffed the prisoner to a bar welded on the dash. After he finished, he picked up his radio's microphone.

"County Two," Early said into it. "Hutch, you out there?"

"Go ahead, Chief," a voice came back.

"Where're you?"

"Coming down Twenty-Four to the cut-over to Leonardville."

"Break it off. It's all over but the shouting."

"Roger that. What do you want me to do?"

"Go on into Manhattan, to the hospital, would you? Tell them we've got a gunshot wound coming in in twenty."

"You've got it."

Early hung the microphone over the mirror at the top of the windshield. "You won't bother that now, will you, Mister Teagan?"

Teagan didn't answer.

"Yes, well, I guess I wouldn't be much for conversation either if someone had put a bullet in me." Early walked away, around to Wells and Frye idling at the back of the Jeep, Frye with two rifles and a nickel-plated revolver. Early motioned at them. "This is the armory, I suppose."

"The deer rifle and revolver," Wells said, "are Boots'. The Springfield's Speed's."

Early helped himself to the deer rifle, a Marlin. He shucked the shells from it and laid the rifle behind the seat, next to a jerry can of gasoline. He looked deep into Frye's eyes as he took the Thirty-Eight from him and shook four shells from the cylinder. "You the other shooter?"

"Yup."

"Do I have to arrest you?"

"I guess."

Wells put a hand on Early's arm. "Speed's my friend. What say I bring him to town tomorrow and we all visit with the county attorney, see if we can figure how to play this out?"

"I can live with that." Early relieved Frye of his rifle. "You don't mind?" he asked as he jacked a live round from the gun's firing chamber and laid the empty weapon in with the others. "Law, what charges should I write up on Teagan?"

"Oh, how about illegal discharge of a firearm and failure to obey a peace officer? That should hold him for the night."

"Good enough. Now come here." Early tugged on a strap of Wells' bib overalls, pulling his reserve deputy down to where he could lift the towel from

Wells' head. Early parted the hair. "Split the skin, all right. Could maybe have even grooved the old head bone. You want to come with me? We can get you sewed up at the hospital."

"No, Jodie can do it. She's a good hand with a needle."

Early placed the towel back on the top of Wells' head and put Wells' hand over the towel. "So I'll see you in the morning?"

"What time?"

"Say nine?" Early slipped back into his Jeep. He fired up the engine and scratched back around to the driveway, waving as he departed. He waved, too, to Jodie and a second woman in Wells' truck slowing for the turn-in.

Frye stared at the new arrivals. "Is that Elvie with Jo?"

"Looks to be."

"Oh gawd, I'm gonna catch hell now."

Wells took the towel from his head, and again he played his fingers along the crease in his scalp. "You and me both."

WELLS AND FRYE, scrubbed and in clean duds–Oshkosh-By-Gosh bib overalls and a white shirt for Wells, the sleeves rolled up to the elbows, and blue twill work pants and shirt for Frye–chugged down the steps to the basement office of the Riley County Sheriff's Department, the bell in the courthouse's clock tower chiming nine.

"You look a bit wilted," Early said as the two came in the door. "Gladys's got a jug of iced tea. Help yourselves while I get Carl down here."

Gladys Morton, a stout woman and Early's secretary for half a decade, took two cups from a side cabinet. She handed them to Wells and Frye.

"You doing all right, Mister Wells?" she asked as she lifted a jar of tea out of the Fridgidaire next to her desk.

"If I don't melt way down south here in the banana lands."

"No, I mean your head."

Wells tilted his head down. "Want to see my wife's needlework?"

Missus Morton punched him. "If you can joke about it, you're all right."

"Guess I am."

She poured the tea, taking care that a goodly amount of ice chips plopped into each cup. "Speaking of the heat, Lowell Jack said on the radio this morning it's going to get up to a hundred and five."

"That makes me want to get back home and go fishin' on the Little Muddy."

"You catch anything, Mister Wells?"

"We got pan fish up there, one makes a meal for four people." He held out his hands, showing something the size of a wash pan. "Wouldn't you say that's true, Speed?"

Frye snickered.

"I'm sorry, Gladys, I don't know where my manners have gone to. This is Speed Frye."

"I figured." She set the jar aside and reached out to shake hands.

"Speed, this is Gladys Morton. She keeps the

deputies honest."

"Not an easy thing to do. It's good to meet you, Mister Frye, but if you'll excuse me, there are some reports I have to type up for the sheriff." The blue-haired woman darted away, first to the refrigerator where she parked the tea jar, then to her desk. There she rolled a form into her typewriter.

Early hung up his telephone. He waved Wells and Frye over to his desk and pointed them to a couple side chairs. A fan overhead stirred air that smelled of damp paper.

Early scratched at his mustache. "Carl'll be right down. Law, what's that rash on your neck?"

"Horse nettle. Got in some yesterday."

"You get down and roll in it?"

"That's just what I did, but it wasn't my choice. How's Boots doin'?"

"Better. He's complaining about the groceries we serve and how thin his mattress is."

"Complaining, that's a good sign."

"Yes, unless he gets my jailer mad at him, then his eats will get as thin as his mattress."

Carl Weiland hurried in from the hallway, the left sleeve of his shirt swinging free at his side. The man had lost an arm on Guadalcanal.

"Law," he said, sticking out his lone hand to shake with Wells. "And this must be Mister Frye."

"Yessir." Frye, too, shook hands with the man who commanded his future.

Weiland pulled a chair over to Early's desk. "I talked to Mister Teagen. Mister Frye, he tells me you tried to kill him."

"I threatened. Seems to me there's a difference."

"Lay it out for me." Weiland waggled his fingers at Early for a notepad. He took a pencil from his shirt pocket and licked the point.

"He beat my daughter," Frye said.

Weiland looked over at Lawton Wells. "That true?"

"Uh-huh. Blacked her eyes. Kicked her in the stomach when she fell. Doc Grafton says she's got three cracked ribs."

"So that happened first?" Weiland asked, scribbling fast.

Frye massaged his chin. "That's right."

"And?"

"She called me at the post office. I work there. Simmie was all panicky, so I went out to her house. Boots made the mistake of hangin' around, so I took an axe handle to him."

Early slid a typed report in front of the county attorney. "Doc Grafton's statement."

Weiland read it. "Oooo, a lot more damage on him than just a hole in the shoulder. So who was shooting at who?"

Frye shifted in his chair. "He got to his rifle and shot out my tires as I was tryin' to leave."

"So you get your gun out and start shooting back?"

"Yessir."

Weiland chewed on his pencil's eraser. "And neither of you can shoot straight enough to hit the other?"

"Lordy man, he shot out two of my tires, brand

new from the Monkey Ward store. He put three holes in the door of my truck and shot my hood ornament off."

Weiland pointed his pencil at Frye. "But he didn't hit you."

"No."

"And you didn't hit him."

Wells interrupted. "Speed had to be more careful. His girl was in the house."

"So we've got the assault of Boots on the girl and your assault on him." Weiland used his empty sleeve to mop at the sweat dribbling down his temple. "Am I the only one to think it's hot in here?"

Early leaned back. He put his feet up on his desk. "Carl, the way I see it, no judge is gonna convict a father for revenging his daughter. And if they get this story down at the Mercury, you'll look darn silly even bringing the charge."

"I have to agree, so here's what we'll do. Mister Teagan shot first, so we charge him with attempted murder." Weiland turned to Wells. "He resist arrest?"

"I told him to give up. He wouldn't."

"So you shot him?"

"Only after he tried to blow my head off. Carl, he was gonna get somebody killed, and I didn't want it to be me."

"Fair enough. I've got a grand jury upstairs. Let's go tell them what happened and get a bill of indictment." Weiland leveled his gaze at Frye. "However this comes out, you're not getting your rifle back. Jimmy, you take that gun down to the junkyard and have it chopped up for scrap."

Frye opened his mouth, but Wells stopped him with a cold stare.

The county attorney gathered up the pad he'd borrowed and pushed his chair back. "One last question."

"What's that?" Early asked as he, too, stood.

"Has this Teagan got any relatives who are going to raise hell?"

Early shifted his gaze to Lawton Wells.

Wells rubbed at the rash on his neck. "He's got a brother."

Weiland clapped a hand of Early's shoulder. "Jimmy, you go find him. Haul him in and throw him so far back in the jail he won't see daylight til this is over. I'm not having anyone else shooting up my county."

Wells continued to rub at his neck. "He's not gonna come easy."

EARLY AND WELLS sat in the weeds, yellow rocket and burdock to either side of them, watching the moon rise over the Flint Hills east of Leonardville.

Early chewed on a blade of bluestem grass. "You sure you want to do it this way?"

Wells pushed his straw hat back onto the back of his head. "Tillman is Boots' big brother in more ways than one. He's wide as a door and mean as a boar hog. We go at him head on, we're either gonna have to kill him or fight him, and I'm too old for fightin' him, and, Cactus, you're too small."

"Sure hope we don't have to wait much longer."

"Your wife at you again?"

"Yeah."

"Well, Mother Nature's a wonderful thing. When the pressure builds, old Tillman will roll himself out of bed and come hustling out to the little house at the end of the path."

"Speaking of pressure, I gotta pee."

"Behind that bush over there. I'll keep watch."

The moon had risen high enough in the sky that it silhouetted an outhouse some twenty yards from Wells and a ramshackle cabin beyond painted puce, a color the Leonardville hardwareman had thrown out because nobody would buy it. Tillman Teagen had rescued a couple cans from the town dump.

A light flicked on. Wells saw it, and he heard the spring on a screen door being stretched and a slap as the spring pulled the door shut.

"He's comin'," he whispered.

Early slouched back, zipping up his pants. "About time."

Wells, on his feet, held a coil of rope. The two made their way out of the weed patch, the sounds of night insects and tree frogs masking their footsteps.

"He got a dog?" Early asked.

"Every dog Till ever had ran off at the first chance."

As they got closer, Wells passed the loop end of his rope to Early. Wells then crept around the outhouse, playing out the rope at waist level while, inside, Tillman Teagen ripped off with a thunderous release of gas, shaking the little building.

Wells, back with Early, pushed his end of the rope through the loop. The two snugged the rope tight and tied it off.

Early dashed away into the night while Wells went around to the front of the outhouse. He pecked on the door. "Till?"

"Who the hell's out there?"

"Lawton Wells."

"The sonuvabitch who shot my brother?"

"Till, it's this way, he shot me first."

Teagen kicked the door, but it didn't yield. "Git away from there! I'm gonna kill you, old man."

"That's what your little brother said and look what it got him."

Teagen slammed into the door. "Let me out of here, sonuvabitch!"

"I might be enticed to think about it."

Teagan slammed into the door a second time.

"Till, how about this? You put your hands out first so I can handcuff 'em. I'll open the door for that. See, the county attorney wants you in jail."

"Not on your life."

"Sorry you feel that way."

Headlights came bouncing across the field, a V-Eight engine howling. Early's Jeep swung around and slid to a stop a dozen paces from the outhouse.

Wells trotted out with the loose end of the rope while Tillman Teagan hammered on the walls and ripped at the boards. Wells looped the rope around the rear bumper of the Jeep and tied it off.

"He sounds kind of mad, huh," Early said.

"Oh, yes. Give him a ride."

Early hauled the gear shifter into first. He stomped on the gas pedal and the rope snapped tight, whanging the outhouse from its foundation. The miniature prison slammed over and bounced, shuddering as its speed came up to that of the retreating Jeep.

Fifty yards on, Early stopped.

Wells strolled up to the outhouse. He tapped on the side. "Ready to give up?"

"Hell no!"

"All right." Wells went on to the Jeep where he climbed into the passenger seat. "He's one tough bird, Cactus. Shall we take him across the ditch?"

Early spun the steering wheel toward the road and let out the clutch. Slowing when he came up on the borrow ditch, he eased the Jeep down through it, then scratched gravel.

The outhouse ripped down into the ditch, hit the up-slope, and flipped end for end, still on the rope.

Wells glanced back. "I'm thinking that should have tamed him some, wouldn't you say?"

Early stopped the Jeep. The two peace officers got out and rambled back to the outhouse that appeared to have no more than a day left in it before it would shed itself of its skin of boards.

"Till?" Wells called out.

No answer.

"You all right in there?"

"I think I busted my beak."

"You give up?"

"Don't want to, but I guess."

"Stick a foot out through the hole then, buddy."

Early turned his flashlight on the underside of the outhouse's bench seat, the seat hole clearly visible.

Out came a bare foot and leg and a torn pant leg.

Wells took a short length of cotton rope from his pocket. He looped it around Teagen's ankle, but before he could pull up on the rope, Teagan kicked back, hit Wells in the chest and sent him sprawling.

"Now you've done it." Wells pushed himself up. He grabbed the rope with both hands and hauled hard, slamming Teagen's butt into the hole.

"Gawddammit that hurts!"

"Oh, does it now? Till, the sheriff's gonna open the door, and you do what he says. If you don't, he got the gawdamnedest biggest gun you've ever seen, and he's just gonna blow your head off and be done with you . . . Well?"

"All right . . . all right."

Wells braced himself. He held his hog-tie rope tight and gave a nod to Early.

Early cut the other rope—the heavier rope—away from the outhouse, and the door fell open. He shined his flashlight inside. "My, son, you are a mess. On your stomach now."

"I can't with him haulin' on my leg."

"Well, do the best you can. Law, give him a little slack."

Wells eased up on the rope.

And Teagen pulled up, flopping on his belly.

"Now be a good boy," Early said. "Put your hands behind you."

One hand came out and back, then the other.

Early leaned in with his handcuffs. "Tillman, how can you stand the stink in here?" He snapped the handcuffs on and dragged Teagen out.

The shackled man shook like an angry bull. He came up and charged Early.

Wells saw it and hauled up on his rope. Out came Teagan's foot, and down he went face first on a bull thistle.

Early stepped on Teagan's back. He braced the barrel of his Forty-Five against the man's head, right behind his ear. "I think I'll just kill him."

Teagan shrieked.

Wells winked at Early. "Go ahead. We'll throw his carcass in the crap pit. Nobody'll ever know."

Early drew the hammer back.

"No! Please. Gawd, don't shoot me."

Wells eased up on the rope. "Cactus, sounds to me like we got us a prisoner here. Want the leg irons?"

September

Sleepless in September
by John

I find myself sleepless in September
Trying to remember… something.
This thing I'm trying to remember is stinging my head.
"Horror!" I shout and shoot up like a spring in my bed.

The thought floods through me,
The terror of me forgetting something like this.
"How could I forget!" I hold myself close.
I cannot fall asleep with my guilty heartbeat.

It is the week after
That I finally remember
In this sleepless September night.
The cage finally opens with a bang and a fright.

"It's nothing." I try to comfort myself.
"Just something in the wind."
But it creeps its way in,
Like a sin.

I hold myself tighter. "How could I forget."
The thought skitters down me like a spider. I shiver.
How could I forget? It was on my mind lately.

But the burden of it weighs down too greatly.

"I know, I'll do it tomorrow." I sigh with relief.
But alas, it was no use for it had passed.
The thing I forgot had gone at last.
And to think I forgot.

I forgot indeed.
And now I can't sleep.
"How could I forget–" I weep and I weep.
"–to write that paper that was due last week."

The Tricksters
by Jerry

"ISN'T THIS QUAINT," I said as I stepped into my grandparents' church for the first time. "I want to have my wedding here."

Oil lamps for lighting, a pump organ, a furnace beneath the floor with the one big register for heat in front of the altar platform, bench seats that were . . . well, we'll put on the invitations "BYOC". Bring your own cushions.

"AND WHO GIVES this young woman?" the minister asked.

My father, a widower—my mom died ten years ago—jumped up, waving. He slapped my hand into my husband-to-be's hand. "Marco," he said in a whisper loud enough to be heard at the back of the church, "you don't know how long I've waited to unload this girl. Hallelujah, and I'll have a check for ya when this thing's over."

My father!

There was giggling and chuckling among the audience.

When he sat down, he sat on a whoopie cushion. BYOC. I know he brought it to embarrass me. And this time there was laughter.

Real laughter.

Loud laughter.

And someone even guffawed. My dad's brother, my uncle!

But at least now I knew I was safe.

However, Dad's cell phone went off during the "I do's," the ring tone *The March of the Toreadors.* "Hello," he shouted into his cell to be heard, "I can't talk now. I'm at my daughter's wedding!"

We made it the rest of the way through the ceremony with no more disasters. The minister pronounced us married, and Marco and I turned and ran down the aisle. Dad stepped out just as we passed him, stepped on my train and the back of my dress ripped out.

My dad did that. My father!

But I got him. As we drove away, I saw him struggling with the handle on the door of his new Tahoe. Before the service, I Gorilla-glued his doors shut—all of four of them and the lift gate, too.

And what's waiting for him when he finally gets a door open? Stink. Three pounds of Limburger cheese and an open jar of sauerkraut that have been locked in there in the baking sun for two hours.

And when he gets home to watch the Packers game, when he sits down in his La-Z-Boy, when he leans back, the back's going to fall all the way to the floor because I rejiggered his lounger.

Surely, when my father gets up, he'll think he's safe now. But I've got one more surprise for him—a snake in his bed. A rubber snake, yes, but he won't know that until after he beats it to death with the baseball bat he keeps in his closet.

October

The Lynn Street Piano Player
by John

I MET BRANDON on the first of October. He was older than me by a good two or three decades, but his demeanor was still that of his twenty-year-old college dropout self. He was happy and he was sad, but, most of all, he was genuine. He was a person who had stories, yet he was more interested in your stories.

The night I met Brandon was a quiet Friday night down on Lynn Street. I was on my way to a party when I heard a few notes from a piano in the distance and someone rambling on over the notes, someone saying, "Hey, we're all here just to get by, but let's all be here to have some fun."

The person—a man—spoke with such passion that I couldn't help but cross the street, just to listen to this guy.

There was a café there with a piano outside, and that's where I came on Brandon—at the keyboard. There wasn't a real audience, just passersby dropping a few coins in a jar he had placed on top of the piano.

But I sat down on a park bench by the piano, to listen.

"Hey, man," he said, his eyes closed, lost in his music, "welcome to tonight. Have you ever been to

Boston?"

"Yeah, I used to live there," I said.

"Well, here's a song about how to get a Boston girl when you've got twenty-to-one odds against ya. It's called *Back Angels.*"

He began with a riff, then flowed into the lyrics, the words he sang seeming like something he had found on treasure hunt. I could tell they meant something to him and only him. Brandon was a decent piano player with a decent voice, but, like they say, some people just have 'it' and Brandon had 'it.'

He sang more of the song, but interrupted himself. "Hey, what does your father do, man?" he asked as he continued to play.

"Well, he was a navy captain for a long while."

"Ah, a captain. So you were a military brat, eh?" He snickered while continuing with the accompaniment. "Oh, the navy captain! God loves a navy man! Tell me something else. Where are you from? You from here or somewhere else?"

"I'm from Wisconsin."

"Wisconsin! Cheese!" He cheered and played *The Beer Barrel Polka.*

I noticed an aura around him, an aura that seemed to suggest nothing bad could ever happen to him as long as he played the piano.

"What a night tonight is, isn't it?" he said, playing on into the chorus. "It's nights like this that I love to play the piano and just be here."

"How long have you been playing?" I asked.

"Oh, about five minutes. Just sat down." He

played on.

"Ah, I see. And where are you from?"

"I'm from wherever will take me in. LA for a while, then San Fran, but it's so hard to live there and play music. It's so expensive. Then I switched coasts to New York, and then Boston where I fell in love and fell out of love, and here I am now in Iowa City."

He played and sang and played some more, all the while talking to me. I never lost interest in his voice, in his music, and I never felt more at home with a stranger. Someone who's been there and learned. Someone who's lived a satisfying life filled with joys and sorrows, too.

"My name is Brandon," he said. "I'm here every now and then. Mostly on Fridays."

He continued playing and ended with an arpeggio as soft as the night.

Brandon sipped the rest of his hot chocolate gone cold. He put on his coat and tipped his cap—a duffer's cap—to me. "Thanks for being my audience."

With that, he wandered off into the night humming a tune he'd probably made up and disappeared.

I'VE WALKED PAST Lynn Street a number of times on Friday nights since, and I haven't seen Brandon there. I wonder if he's traveled somewhere else or if maybe a music producer discovered him. The piano still remains there outside the café, hardly ever touched now. Yet there are Friday nights when I'm passing by that I hear a voice say, "Hey, we're all here just to get by, but let's all be here to have some fun."

The Fly-By-Night Towing & Recovery Service
by Jerry

MORTY BROWN HOWLED, finger-combing his hazel mane back from his face as he watched his partner chalk Cheetah/Chevy 1963 on the side of their tow truck. "Snatching cars, it's the best gig we've ever had!"

Ceril Vaskos, as hairy as Brown, only blonde, drew a line under Cheetah. "Ain't it so? But this guy just made it too easy."

"Yeah, fell for that old coupon-under-the-windshield-wiper trick: Present this at Buffalo Hot Wings for an all-you-can-eat meal free."

"While he stuffed himself inside, we hooked up to his car outside and hauled ass."

Brown's cell vibrated. He grubbed it out of his back pocket and swiped a paw across the screen. "Text message here. Boss wants us to grab a Demon." He turned the cell to Vaskos.

Vaskos scanned the screen and grinned. "Interesting. Little Beelzebubby Junior is behind in his payments again. Where do you think we can catch him this time?"

"It's Friday night, a full moon out, our kinda night. I'd say we'll find him cruising The Circuit."

"Then let's go get us a Demon."

Brown glanced at his cell's screen. He tapped a couple commands, bringing up eBay. "Demon, Dodge, Nineteen Seventy-One, there's one listed here for thirty-two thousand nine."

He tapped again at the screen and whistled at the result.

Vaskos looked over as he capped his wide-tipped chalker. "Whaddaya got?"

"The Barrett-Jackson auction site. Demons mint condition, they've sold them for forty-four thousand. Ten percent, that makes our payday, say, four thousand four."

"Not bad for an hour's work. Shall we?" Vaskos went for the driver's door of their hopped-up Kenworth tricked out with all the goodies for towing everything from a Smart Car to a massive sixty-five-foot long Mack Bulldog tractor-trailer.

Vaskos fired up the big snorter and pulled away from the Wreckit Finance Company's storage yard–Wreckit, formerly Scrooge & Marley and now owned by the conglomerate Hades Inc.

Brown, in the shotgun seat, scrolled down his screen. "Here's one, Vas," he said.

"What's that?"

"Why was the werewolf arrested at the butcher shop?"

Vaskos puzzled that over, but headlights flashed up on his windshield, breaking his concentration. A car streaked by, and he caught sight of it, its silhouette and taillights, enough to tell him it was a Chevy Impala and new. "Didn't we grab one of those last week?"

Brown glanced across the cab. "Impala? Yup, thirty-five hundred for that one. But you're avoiding my question. Why was the werewolf arrested at the butcher shop?"

"I give up."

"Because he was caught chop lifting!" Brown cackled as he went back to his screen. "All right now, what do you get when you cross a werewolf with a hyena?"

Vaskos hit the clicker and cranked the wheel of the big rig to the right, turning off One Hundred Twenty-Fifth Street onto Wisconsin Boulevard. "Cross a werewolf with a hyena? Can't say I've ever dated a hyena. I don't know."

"I don't know, either, but if it laughs, I'll join in!" Brown slapped the dashboard and hooted, bouncing in his seat.

Vaskos stared at him. "Where are you getting these werewolf things?"

"I Love Werewolves dot Com." Brown turned his screen to his partner, but only for a moment, then he went back to it. "How about this? What parting gift did the werewolf parents give their son when he left home?"

"That one I know, a comb."

"Aw, you sure can spoil a joke." Brown, no longer bouncing, no longer hooting, sulked on his side of the cab.

Vaskos gestured ahead. "Look sharp. There's the K-mart. The circuit starts here."

A gaggle of teens and early twenty-somethings

lounged by a flock of cars and pickups—a number of pickups with oversized tires and jacked-up suspensions—in the K-mart parking lot by the exit, a glut of them leaving as others arrived. Those leaving pulled out onto the boulevard and headed west, plugging all three lanes as drivers challenged one another for positions in the parade.

Vaskos slipped over into the outside lane and gave two toots on his tow truck's airhorn. When the driver of the GMC pickup next to him looked up, Vaskos fist punched the air.

The driver responded. He kicked his truck into neutral and tromped on the accelerator twice, popped his truck back into road gear, and rolled coal, blasting out a cloud of diesel smoke as his swung away into the lane to his left and sped off.

Brown jabbed his partner. "You gonna let him get away with that?"

"Nope." Vaskos powered the Kenworth into the inside lane in pursuit, closing on the GMC driver idling at the next traffic light. As the light changed, Vaskos pulled into the center lane and shot past the GMC driver, cut back in front of him, and snapped a switch down that threw his exhaust from the twin stacks to twin pipes under his truck's chassis. Vaskos floored the accelerator, rolling coal of his own, smoking the Jimmy driver.

Brown, watching the cruising traffic out his side window, slapped back at Vaskos. "There he is."

"Who?"

"Bellzy. Man, look at that Demon—yellow and black, twin air scoops on the hood, an airfoil on the back. Get him!"

Vaskos muscled the bellowing Kenworth into the center lane and slowed as he came up beside the Demon. He flicked on his light bar, setting off blue and white hazard lights that traveled the length of the bar and back, repeating their cycle. Vaskos shot his trigger finger at the driver of the Demon, and, when the driver—Beelzebub Junior—glanced his way, Vaskos jerked his thumb at the side of the road.

Beelzebub and the girl in his passenger seat glared up at Vaskos, lips curled. He stomped the Demon's accelerator to the firewall, the rear tires tearing, spinning, burning off tread as the car fishtailed away into the night, cutting in and out of ever more distant traffic.

Brown drummed his fingers on the dashboard. "That didn't go well, did it?"

"Nope. One thing's sure."

"What's that?"

"He's not gonna stay on the street. He's gonna hide. He doesn't want Daddy taking his wheels back."

"So where do we look now?"

"I don't know." Vaskos held to the steering wheel, glancing from side to side through the gloom as they passed an O'Charlie's, a Ted's Big-and-Tall Shop, a Red Lobster, and a Hooters. "Hooters, hmm. He could park out back, but we'd still see his car."

Beyond Hooters, they came up on a used car lot, the sign out front proclaiming 'Honest Ed's. One hundred one cars priced right.' Vaskos rubbed his well-whiskered chin. "This is it. You want to hide a car? You hide it in plain sight."

He slowed the big rig and turned in at the end driveway, dropped the transmission down to second and motored along the miniature world of well-used but highly-polished vehicles parked three deep. Vaskos snapped on his spotlight. He played it over the cars, moving the light from rank to rank, front row, middle, and back. "There."

The light bathed a black and yellow car in the back row–the Demon. It shot backwards out of the row, swung around and sped off in the direction opposite the Kenworth, took air at the exit and banged down onto the boulevard in front of a patrol car. The Demon raced away with the patrol car after it, lights flashing and siren whooping.

Vaskos watched in his side mirror. "He belongs to the cops now."

Brown hunkered down on his side of the cab. He tapped away on his cell's screen. "No payday for us on that one. Might as well get in a couple rounds of Giddy Up Mix-up."

Vaskos, incredulous, let the Kenworth roll to a stop. "My Little Pony? You're still hung up on that game?"

Brown's cell jumped in his hand, vibrating. He punched the text message command and scrolled down to the latest. "It's the boss, again."

"He's found out already that his boy got away?"

"Nope, but he's got another car he wants us to grab, a 'Sixty-Four Shelby Cobra, a hard-top coupe worth a pile."

"He's got an address for it?"

"It's way out in Mukwonago, the land of many

bears."

Vaskos, an eyebrow rising, gave his partner a puzzled look.

Brown scrunched his shoulders as he turned up his palms. "Mukwonago, I read it somewhere. It's a Pottawatomie word, means the land of many bears."

"Oookay, so punch the address into the GPS, and let's go see if the owner left his snake in the driveway."

A COUPLE TURNS and Vaskos guided the Kenworth onto the entrance ramp and down onto the I-road, heading west. Twenty-five miles and he cut off at the Mukwonago exit. There he negotiated the tow truck through a rat's maze of secondary roads and residential streets until a feminine voice on the GPS announced "One block to destination. Destination on left."

Vaskos shifted down. He slowed and puttered past the address, motioning out his window. "There's the snake."

Brown, gleeful, punched him. "We gonna back in and hook up?"

Vaskos wheeled off to the side of the street. "Too much noise. We'd likely have the owner on us before we could get out of the driveway."

"So whadda we do?"

"Buddy, you've always wanted to drive a Cobra. Are you up for a screamin' ride in a widow maker?"

Brown reached under the truck's seat and produced a Slim Jim—a jimmy stick. With a giant grin, he showed it to Vaskos who gave him a thumbs-up.

Brown jumped down from the high seat of the Kenworth and ran, crouched low, thinking that surely would hide him from anyone who might be looking out their windows. He scuttled up the sidewalk to the driveway and scooted in beside the driver's door of the Cobra, snagging his shirt sleeve on the rose hedge that bordered the driveway. Weird, he thought as he tugged at his sleeve, someone who drives a super-sizzler of a car tending roses. Go figure. He ripped his sleeve free and hunkered down. Brown forced himself to slow his breathing, to steel his nerves. After some moments, he eased himself up, taking care not to get caught on the roses' thorns again, eased himself up just enough that he could peer over the hood of the car at the house.

Hmm, no lights in any of the windows. A dog barking, a little yapper by the sound of it. Must be a couple houses away. I wonder if this guy's got a dog. Just as long as it's not a pit bull.

Brown pushed himself up the rest of the way and slipped his Slim Jim in between the driver's door glass and the gasket seal. He slid the jimmy stick down ever so slowly into the window well where he maneuvered it, where he fished with it, feeling for the rod that would release the door lock. He hooked the rod—felt like it, yes, he was sure of it—and, pursing his lips, he pulled up.

The lock button popped.

Brown shot a 'we are number one' finger into the air. Then he brought the jimmy stick up and out, and with it came a tangle of wires.

Damn.

One shorted—sparking—setting off the car's alarm.

And the headlights.

And the running lights.

The racket and flashing, Brown threw himself inside the Cobra. He dove under the dash and fumbled for the right wires to cross, to fire up the big-block engine, all four hundred twenty-seven cubic inches of it.

He found the wires and, with shaking fingers, touched them together.

The engine rumbled to life.

Brown mopped the sweat from his forehead. He came up . . . and blanched.

On the front steps of the house stood a man in boxer shorts and nothing else–the snake's owner? had to be–the man wielding a Colt King Cobra, a Magnum Forty-Four. Brown recognized the gun, the gun pointed at him, the man screaming something. Brown dove again, and a blast blew out the windshield.

The scene lit up. Brown glanced back to see the Kenworth's spotlight aimed his way. He sneaked a peek over the dash and saw the shooter shading his eyes against the hot light, squinting, angling for a second shot. Brown slammed the snake into reverse. He burned rubber all the way down the driveway and wheeled into a turn that carried him in reverse past the Kenworth. Brown whipped the car around, clutched and rammed the transmission into first gear, and raced away with the rear tires smoking, Vaskos after him, shifting up to keep up. At the end of the block, Brown swung right.

His cell went off, the ring tone five bars of Prokofiev's Peter and the Wolf. Brown scratched the handset icon before he tossed the cell onto the seat beside him. "Vas?" he hollered at his cell.

"Yeah. You all right?"

"Other than I need a change of underwear? Do you know where the hell the kill switch is for the alarm?"

"Should be under the dash on the left."

Brown felt for it, found a button, and pressed it, and the honking horn ceased honking. He blew out his cheeks, relieved.

Vaskos came back on the cell. "Can you make it back to the yard or do you want me to tow you?"

"Man, I'm drivin'. This car's wild. "

"Know the way back to the Interstate?"

"Hell, no."

"I've got the route up on my GPS. Lemme pass you."

Brown touched the brakes, and the Kenworth powered on by.

BROWN SETTLED IN on the Interstate, steering with one hand, enjoying the wind in his face, putting his tongue out to slurp up the occasional night insect. With his free hand, he thumbed at commands on his cell's screen and brought up a site that contained a wealth of technical data on the Cobra. "Vas," he said to his cell.

"I'm here."

"Do you know how fast this thing is?"

"Zero to a hundred and back in thirteen point nine seconds."

"That, too. But it says here, right here, that flat out this car can do a hundred sixty-five mph. A hundred sixty-five, man."

A whistle came back from Vaskos plus a question. "You thinking of putting your foot in the carburetor?"

"No, but if I did, no cop could catch me." Brown checked his mirror. "Speaking of cops, you see what I see? Flashing lights behind me maybe a half mile and headlights burning up on my bumper."

A car shot past in the passing lane. "Damn, it's the devil's kid. The Demon can do a hundred and a quarter. The cops'll never catch him, but I can."

"You're not thinking—"

"I'm thinking the two cars we've got—and this one, the Cobra's worth a half-mil minimum—plus with the Demon, we've got us sixty thousand dollars comin'. That's worth goin' for, an' I'm goin' for it." Brown floored the accelerator. The car, already at seventy, scorched the pavement as he swung it out into the passing lane and raced away from the Kenworth.

A hundred forty and Brown saw the Demon's taillights. A hundred sixty and he streaked past the car, tromped on the brakes, the massive disks hauling down the speed almost as fast as the gas pedal had forced it up. Brown threw the Cobra into a sideward skid, blocking both lanes of his side of the Interstate. He held to the steering wheel, riding the skid, the

Demon closing.

The Demon cut away toward the inside shoulder, ran off the road, and went airborne. It splashed down in a swale in the median, the swale filled with cattails and swamp water. A wave went up into the opposing lanes.

Brown idled the Cobra off onto the shoulder. He got out and parked his butt on the car's front fender, his arm's folded across his chest. From there, Brown watched Beelzebub Junior heft himself out of the driver's window of the Demon, watched him slog around, half dazed, to the other side of the car and wrench the passenger door open, watched him pull the girl out.

Three police cars skidded up, their sirens cycling down–a state trooper's car, a sheriff's car, and a Mukwonago P.D. cruiser. All the drivers bailed out and two ran down into the median, their guns drawn–the trooper and the Mukwonago officer.

The third–a deputy sheriff toting a long-barreled Maglite–shambled over to Brown. "What happened here?" he asked, aiming the beam of his Mag out into the swale.

Brown shrugged.

The officer brought the light back and shined it in Brown's face. He stared at him, then moved the light to the windshield, most of the glass gone. The deputy gave a jerk of his head toward the windshield. "What happened to that?"

"Well," Brown said, "I'm in the repo business. The owner didn't like me taking his car, so he shot out the window."

The officer poke his light into the interior, crumbles of shattered glass on the passenger seat and the floor refracting the light. "Uh-huh. Sir, was he trying to shoot you?"

"Likely."

"And I should believe this, why?"

Brown gestured up the highway, at the big tow truck rolling up, its light bar a blizzard of blue and white. "My partner, he's got the paperwork. The file came in on my cell, and I sent it to the printer in our truck."

The door opened, and Vaskos stepped down from the Kenworth.

Brown hollered to him, "The paperwork on the Cobra, our friend here wants to see it."

Vaskos reached back and brought out a manila folder. While he hiked over to Brown and the deputy, he sorted through his repossession orders. "This is the one you want to see," he said and handed a paper to the deputy.

The deputy put his Mag on the page and read. "All right, the car's yours. Now the Demon down in the swamp—"

"That's ours, too." Vaskos gave the deputy a second paper.

Again he read. "Just curious, what's the Demon worth?"

"Forty grand, give or take."

"And this one, the Cobra?"

"A half mil."

The deputy pouched out his cheeks in a silent whistle.

"And it's one of the cheap ones," Vaskos said. "A Super Cobra built for the man who designed the Cobra line—Carroll Shelby—last year that one went for five point three mil at auction. I looked it up."

"Unbelievable." The deputy handed the papers back. He peered at the two repo drivers. "You fellas ever think of shaving?"

The other officers trudged up out of the median, marching Beelzebub Junior and the young woman before them, both bejeweled with handcuffs.

"Can you believe it," the trooper said to the deputy, "this guy says we can't arrest him because he's the devil's son or some such."

Vaskos shook his head. "Officer, the stories people will tell to get out of a ticket." He slipped away and up beside Beelzebub and whispered in his ear. "Greetings from your daddy."

Beelzebub twisted his face into a sneer. "Go to hell," he said.

"Ooo, that's not nice. You want my partner and I should tell him where he can find you?"

"He can go to hell, too."

"Well, if your daddy should decide to, he's got nice clean wheels to drive there—yours."

November

Johnny and Mary and the Star That Fell Down
by John

A BEAUTIFUL EVENING, not a cloud in the sky to mask the first star winking on. Was it Polaris? Johnny and Mary watched it, watched its brightness grow as they strolled along in the park, Mary's hand in Johnny's.

For November, the air was remarkable, neither holding the warmth of late fall nor offering up the crispy cold of early winter, right, though, for a cup of hot chocolate. Johnny and Mary settled on a bench, and he unscrewed the top on the Thermos he had carried in his shoulder pack and poured the steaming brew into cups that she held.

They sipped and drew faces in the foam on their drinks and laughed at the stories each told.

They kissed and gazed at one another and kissed some more. Such a perfect world.

A flash as bright as a July sun interrupted, startling Johnny and Mary. They looked up, shaded their eyes as the flash faded to a glow, a red glow.

The ground rumbled.

A subway train passing beneath them?

A precursor to an earthquake?

Mary stared at her hands. "I think we should break up," she said.

"What?"

"I said I think we should break up."

The rumble increased. A building across the way swayed. The red glow in the eastern sky, moments before an object the size of a fist, increased to that of a soccer ball.

Johnny looked away from Mary. "What makes you say we should break up?"

"I just feel unenthused in this relationship."

"Unenthused, what does that mean?"

Before she could answer, he felt the air go hot.

The ball of red, you could see it now hurtling toward the earth, the wind whipping up, fires breaking out in the distance.

Mary moved away. "I'm so sorry, Johnny," she said over her shoulder.

"Wait, Mary! Please!"

She stopped.

She swivelled around, slowly.

He stared into her eyes, her eyes tearing up, yet he felt safe in them.

A nearby street lamp exploded.

The trees nearest ignited, flaming up like torches.

The wind became a gale.

Yet the two stood transfixed, gazing at one another.

Mary's eyes fell out of love with Johnny's.

Johnny's eyes fell more in love with Mary's.

And a star fell down from the sky and swept the two lovers away.

A November Story
by Jerry

Derek Wilson
Mrs. Engstrom's class
Marshall Middle School
November 29

How to cook a turkey

Thanksgiving at our house, Dad cooks the turkey, barbecues it usually, but not this year.

This year, he got one of those deep-fat fryers—they were on sale at the Ace hardware store—because deep-fat fryers cook turkeys really fast. The tag said an hour for a 20-pound bird.

One hour!

Well, what developed was a competition with Mr. Hartog, our neighbor. It always does when Dad cooks out in the driveway. They were both giving each other evil looks as they poured the oil in their cookers, and on three, they lit their fires.

While the oil came to a boil, Dad rubbed his secret mix of seasonings on the turkey which he said Mr. Hartog would never guess what they were. He massaged them in and massaged them some more, then he got out this big needle and syringe and shot the legs and breast up with habanero sauce. Buffalo hot wings, Dad said, wasn't going to have anything on his turkey.

By this time the oil was boiling, so Dad lowered the turkey in. He set the cover over the cooker, and, since Mom was in charge of everything else for Thanksgiving dinner, he said we should go inside and watch the Packers/Bears pre-game show.

We got kinda wrapped up in it, I guess, so much so that Mom had to come in and shake Dad and tell him to go out and check on the turkey, that it'd been cooking for an hour and ought to be done.

So we did.

Smoke was rolling out from around the edges of the fryer's cover. Dad, with an oven mitt, lifts the cover off, to see what's going on with our birdie-bird, and a ball of flame shoots up out of there 20 feet in the air. I mean wow! Singed off Dad's mustache and eyebrows and smudged his face.

Mr. Hartog, taking out this perfectly browned turkey from his cooker, cackled and hollered, "You look like the devil, Wally Bob." And I guess Dad did.

Anyway, Dad let loose of that cover. He flung it away like it was a frisbee he didn't want around anymore and it flew off toward Mr. Hartog's kitchen window. It smashed right through it.

Before Mr. Hartog could run over and yell at Dad, a fire truck raced up and a bunch of firemen bailed out and smothered the flame in Dad's cooker with foam. Someone had called 9-1-1. "Weren't we here last Christmas," one of them asked, "when you set your tree on fire?"

Dad said yes and gave them a bottle of Jack

Daniel's and made them promise not to talk about it.

When Dad finally got to carve the turkey–it got kind of black in the fire–the foam must have given it a strange taste because, when Mom tried a bite, she made this awful face and spit the bite in the sink. She shagged Dad out to the garage and told him to get out the grill, that he was making hamburgers.

December

The Man on the Other Side of the Moon
by John

CAPTAIN'S LOG: Sunday, December 25th, 1972.

We, or should I say I, have been in lunar orbit for about 45 minutes now. It seems a lot longer. No more coms for another 20 minutes until I reach the day side of the moon again.

It's Christmas today, if you couldn't tell by the date. I've been in space for several weeks now. Nobody tells you that, when you get this far away from Earth, there's only your crew to talk to and whoever is running the coms down in Houston. But today, it's a day off for most people. So all I have to listen to is the beeps and blips of the electronics in the cockpit and, when we orbit back around to the landing zone, my crew.

This is not an easy day to be alone, especially for a Bostonian away from his church and his family, and even harder knowing that the baseball season is farther away than I am from Earth. Each day I'm away from my La-Z-Boy is a day not worth living. My living room feels like a distant memory. I can't remember the feeling of a hug. Zero gravity has a way of making everyday things feel more and more like fantasies. The farther away you are from home, the farther away the memories.

I miss standing showers.

I miss sleeping lying down.

I miss daytime.

I miss nighttime.

I miss my family.

I miss the Red Sox.

I'll be home soon, I hope, sitting in my La-Z-Boy and watching the Sox . . .and I'll miss the moon even more.

One Alone
by Jerry

HE STOOD SHIVERING in the bus shelter, he in his
mack with the hoodie pulled up, camo cargo pants
and boots, waiting for the 9:20, the last bus running
from the mall to downtown. With nothing to do
other than try to keep warm, he peered up at the
snowflakes dancing and twirling their way down
through a yellowish cone of light from a nearby street
lamp, mesmerized by nature's ballet.

A car rolled by splashing up slush, soaking his
pant legs. He jumped back, too late. Surely some fool
in a hurry to get to the Culver's up the street for a
flavor of the day before the restaurant's closing time,
he thought.

A horn blatted.

He turned toward the sound, a set of headlights
coming his way, the headlights of a big honker of a
vehicle—the Big Blue People Shaker.

The Shaker slowed as it sidled up to the shelter,
air hissing out of the bus' leveler, lowering the front
of the vehicle several inches most particularly for the
handicapped and the elderly.

The door opened and hot air whooshed out, the
air smelling of diesel fumes and an overworked
heater.

The driver, a hefty woman in a fur-collared jacket and ball cap, waved him aboard. "Sorry to be runnin' late, Andy. Hope you not been waitin' long."

Andreo 'Andy' Delio dropped his dollar in the chute that carried the fare down to a toll box beneath the floor. "Just a couple minutes, Babe. Only warmed my anticipation for seeing you."

"Bet you say dat to all us women drivers."

He smiled, a tired smile, and drifted back to a seat on the starboard side. Further back—all the way back—a trio of teen girls, surrounded by packages, tapped away at their cells' screens while gabbing together and giggling. Forward of him sat an old couple, on the port side, clutching Christmas shopping bags on their laps, both stone-faced silent.

The Shaker started up, so Delio settled in to sleep, knowing the driver would wake him before his stop.

But several minutes in, The Shaker slowed, then halted—an unscheduled stop. He sensed it and nudged up an eyelid in time to see two guys coming up the steps, both in hoodies—black, not like his, brown. The one in front brought a pistol out from his waistband and shoved it in the driver's face.

"Gimme yer money now," he said.

The driver stared at him. "What kinda fool you are, funderbutt? Look down dere—" She tipped her head toward the chute. "—da fare money's in a locked box unner da floor. I cain't get it, an' you cain't either."

"Yer own money, then, old lady."

"Well, now, you jus' hep yourself. Wallet's on da

dash. All dat's in it is my CDL."

"No dead presidents? No plastic?"

"Huh-uh."

"Yer watch and cell, then."

"Don't have neither, not on my paycheck."

"Bitch." He wheeled on his partner and thrust him down the aisle. "Get theirs. Clean 'em out."

The partner dug out his own gun as he neared the old couple.

Delio decided he'd had enough, so he let his one open eye close and his chin dip down until it rested on his chest. He started counting the seconds. At twenty-four, he felt a gun barrel prod his shoulder.

"Yo, you. I want yer stuff."

A second prod came. And a third.

"Hey, I think dis guy's dead."

Delio sensed the wannabe bad boy had looked away. With the quickness of a snake striking, he grabbed the front of the man's sweatshirt and yanked him down, rammed his head into the wall, leaving him in a heap. Delio snatched up the man's gun and rolled out into the aisle, training the pistol on the first robber. "Buddy," he said, his voice a poor imitation of Clint Eastwood, "I've been in two wars. I'm a dead shot. You sure you wanna go against me?"

"To hell wid you!"

The robber tensed.

Delio saw it, knew what was next and jacked off the first shot, the bullet smashing through the man's gun hand and ripping up his arm before he could feel the searing pain and react.

Delio raced forward. He threw the robber on the

floor. "Babe, whatcha got I can tie him with?"

She thrust a scarf into his hand, and he bound the robber's hands behind his back, one of the hands bloody, the robber yelping.

Delio slapped him in the back of the head. "Dumb ass. You're lucky you're not dead." He glanced up at the teens in the back. "Call nine-one-one."

Delio, done with his tying chores, rolled away to the driver. "Babe, I've never been here. I don't need the attention. You don't know me or my name."

He scrambled down the steps. Outside, in the snow, he ran to a curbside trash can. There he wiped the gun free of fingerprints and threw it in. When Delio had the driver's eye, he motioned at the trash can and trotted off into the gloom, the wail of a police siren—music of the night—coming from the direction of the city center.

"KINDA LATE, aren'tcha?" the man on the door said as he stepped aside for Delio.

Delio pushed his way on in. He stopped under the glow of an overhead light and stamped the snow from his boots. "Bud, it's not a half-bad night out there."

"Hell, man, it's snowing."

"Not that much, so I went for a walk on the river trail. It's quiet."

"Yup, well, I guess quiet's good for the soul. Hey, there was a robbery and shootout on a city bus tonight. Heard it on the police scanner. You know about that?"

Delio shrugged.

"Well, anyway I kept your room for ya. Here's the key."

The key was a card with a magnetic strip on it, making the rooms at The Homeless Hilton, as Delio called the place, more secure than if they had key locks on the doors.

He took the card and went on upstairs. There he flopped his butt down on his bed and shucked himself out of his mack. Delio saw something—a hole in the side of his coat and a second, an entrance and an exit. He fingered them, wondered about them.

He'd heard only one shot—his, he thought.

He raised his shirt and touched his fingers to his side.

DELIO SAT on a bench in the mall employees' locker room, tucking the cuffs of his Santa pants into the tops of his boots.

His supervisor came swinging around the corner, a white beard in his hand at his side. "Deal, how long you been here?"

Delio kept tucking. "Three weeks."

"In that time you sure haven't said much about yourself."

"Not much to say."

The supervisor held up the beard. "I had the girls in our beauty salon wash and style it for you. Looks pretty good, don't you think?"

Delio took it and hooked the loops over his ears. He adjusted the elastic until he had a tight fit, then put on his square Santa glasses and checked the beard in the mirror behind the supervisor. "Bobby, thanks for this. You're a good man, no matter what the others say."

"What?"

"Nothing."

The supervisor took Delio's place on the bench. He parked his elbows on his knees and watched his Santa pull on his fur-edged red jacket. "Your line-'em-up elf, she's gotta quit tonight. Know anyone we could get on short notice to take her place?"

Delio peered in the mirror at the supervisor. "I might."

"Can you get her in here before your shift starts tomorrow afternoon?"

"Probably."

"Probably's not good enough."

"All right, she's not working anywhere else, so, yes."

"Deal, I'll see that you get a finder's fee if she turns out to be any good."

"How much?"

"Twenty-five bucks."

"Make it thirty." He put on his wig and his Santa hat, shifting the hat to the side until he had it at a jaunty angle. "So Viv's quitting. How come?"

"Oh, her husband's taken a turn for the worst. She says she's gotta be home with him. You know how these things happen."

"Yeah, life has a way of busting in. Bobby, I've gotta get out on the throne. Children will be waiting for jolly old Saint Nick."

"Uh-huh. By the way, how old are you, Nick? You didn't list your birthday on your job app."

"Federal regs. You and the mall can't ask me that. But I'm fifty-six."

The supervisor raked his fingers up the sides of his head, through his hair, fluffing out his mane. "My dad tells me that's a good age. I guess I'll find out in another twenty-eight years."

"Yup, Bobby, you're still a kid. If you're nice to the end of the season, on my last day I'll let you sit on Santa's lap, even let the photo elf take a picture of you and me."

DELIO RAPPED on the door of The Homeless Hilton's room 213, the light above him flickering. It ffsssted and went out.

Delio, still in his mack, rapped again. "Alice, you in there?"

He heard slippers slapping across the tile floor toward the door, that followed by the sound of a deadbolt sliding.

The door opened a couple inches revealing the chain latch still in place, a TV illuminating the inside of the room. An eye appeared above the chain.

Delio pushed his hoodie back off his head. "Alice, you all right?"

"Just watchin' Skin Wars on the Game Channel."

"Skin Wars?"

"Body painting, Deal. Third season for the show. The winner gets a hundred thou."

"Sweetie, it's not gonna be you or me. You gonna let me in?"

She unlatched the chain and opened the door.

The room, stuffy, gave off the air of stale

cigarette smoke. The Homeless Hilton was, by city regulation, smoke-free and booze-free. A violation of either could get a resident bounced.

Delio gandered around.

"I smoke outside," Alice Ferrell said. "It gets on my clothes."

"So the smell comes inside with you. All right, are you sober?"

"You're damn direct."

"Well, are you?"

She shuffled back into the kitchenette. "I've not had a beer in a week, and I go to my meetings."

He peered at her, at her back. "How're you doing for money?"

"The truth?"

"The truth."

She twisted around and leaned against the counter. "Well, I'm a couple feet shy of desperate."

"Your disability check?"

"It's late. Again. You wanna sit down?"

Delio helped himself to a folding chair at the card table that served as the kitchenette's table. In a corner on a rolling stand, a tall blonde on the TV's screen introduced a new contestant.

Ferrell turned the set off. She went to the hot plate for the coffeepot. This she held out to Delio. "Want some?"

"Still making your famous Navy coffee?"

"Thick enough to cut."

"Then slice me off a half a cup."

Ferrell partially filled a hard-used, grungy Melmac cup and topped off a second. The partially filled she set in front of Delio.

He gazed at its blackness. "Is this the real stuff or decaf?"

She laughed, laughed hard, and took the folding chair opposite Delio.

"Alice, I've got a job for you, and you can't say no."

"I FEEL SILLY," she said as she curtsied in her elf's costume before Delio, he in his Santa togs and beard.

"Ho-ho-ho, get over it," he said in his best Santa voice. "The money's good. Now let's go over this one last time."

Alice Ferrell fished in the bag on her belt and brought out a pad of sticky notes and a pen. "I patrol the line of waiting kids and parents, and I talk to them and tell them they won't have to wait long."

"And when you see I'm about finished with the child on my lap?"

"I go to the first kid in the line and get his or her name from the parent. I write it on a Post-It to give to the photo elf, then I bring the kid to you and I say, 'Santa, this is' and I give you the kid's name, and I tell you he or she's been good this year and go back to patrolling the line."

"See? It's easy."

"If you like kids, but, dammit, Deal, I hate kids."

"Not today you don't."

He took her by the elbow and guided her down the hall toward the entrance to Santa Land, but she broke away. "I forgot my coffee. Be back in a sec."

ELF ALICE TOOK a nod from Santa and hurried to the head of the line of anxious children and concerned parents. "And your kid's name is?" she asked the first mother.

"John Smith."

"It's been a long afternoon, ma'am. Really? John Smith?"

The boy, a CPA look-alike in a suit and tie, his necktie askew, puffed himself up. "I am the real John Smith," he said, "and I'm nine years old."

She wrote his name on her pad. "All right, Johnny."

"John. I'm John Smith."

She rubbed her forehead above one eye, squinting. "Yes, John. John Smith. Let me take you to Santa. He's just about ready for you."

Together, they marched to the throne where Santa sent a little girl on her way clutching a candy cane.

Santa gazed up at his elf. "And who do we have here?"

The boy squared himself up Army-straight. "You don't remember me? I was here last year. And the year before. I thought you knew every child."

Elf Alice palmed her sticky note into Santa's gloved hand. He glanced at the note. "Sometimes I forget, but you I do remember." He palmed the note back and put his hands on the boy's shoulders. "You're John Smith."

"The real John Smith," the boy said.

"Yes, so you told me last year and the year before, the real John Smith. Would you like to sit on Santa's lap and have your picture taken with me?"

"I'm too old to sit on your lap, but I'll stand beside you."

Santa moved the boy around to his side. He put his arm around the boy's shoulders and pointed to a camera attached to a screen and a computer, the photo elf, a string bean of a woman, at the ready.

She banged off a picture. "How about another?" she asked. "And in this one, Santa, would you tilt your head toward the boy–"

"John Smith," the boy announced.

"Yes, toward Master Smith. That's it." She shot a second photo and, after she looked at the image on her screen, waved an okay.

Santa drew the boy closer. "Tell me, John Smith, what do you want for Christmas?"

The boy brought out an iPhone. "I've made a list. I have it right here."

He tapped the screen.

Elf Alice slipped away, behind the throne, and sucked in a swallow from her Starbuck's cup.

SANTA HELD a wimpering child out to Elf Alice. "Got a leaker here. Take her back to her mother and get me a towel before you bring the next kid up."

THE PHOTO ELF placed a card on a tripod near the head of the waiting line, the card announcing SANTA MUST FEED HIS REINDEER. HE'LL BE BACK IN 10 MINUTES.

"Really?" one mother asked. "We've already been waiting ten minutes."

The elf eased in close to the questioner. "The truth is Santa has a bladder problem. He has to go to the bathroom."

The mother looked down at her three small ones. "I guess we can wait a little longer, can't we?"

"Mommy, do we have to?" one asked.

The elf hurried away to Santa coming down from his throne. "If I had told them this was your coffee break, they would have rioted. So I told them you had to hit the head."

"They bought it?"

"Yes, they did."

"Elf Connie, you are a con, true to your name, an A-number-one con."

They went around the throne, toward the exit, but Delio stopped when he saw his line-'em-up elf behind the throne, tossing back a swallow from her Starbuck's. He snatched her cup away. "Alice, you're slurring your words. What have you got in here?"

He peered into the cup, the contents—what little that was left—clear, not black. "Vodka?" he asked.

She gave off a pitiful look, like a dog that had been kicked. "I needed a bracer to get me through."

"Bracer, hell. Alice, you're going home sick. If Bobby had caught you, he'd have fired your fanny. And when you get home, call your sponsor."

"But, Deal—"

"The only butt here is yours. Get it back in the program. Connie will cover for you the rest of the night."

DELIO BANGED on the door of 213. "Alice, you in there?"

When no response came, he hauled the Homeless Hilton's night manager forward, the night manager clutching a key card. He slid it into the slot beneath the door's handle.

The lock clicked, and the night manager pushed the door open.

"Alice!" Delio called out as he barged in. He gazed around the room, the room as disheveled as he had often seen its occupant. "Damn, she's not here. Bud, I need to use your office phone to call the police."

The night manager threw up his hands. "Waste o' time, man. She's a drunk. They're not gonna do nuthin'."

"Maybe, maybe not. I still need to use your phone." Delio turned and hustled out of the room and down the stairs to the office, the door open and the night manager behind him.

Delio helped himself to the desk phone. After he consulted a card he took from his shirt pocket, he punched in a string of numbers and waited, eying the night manager. "You got a number for her sponsor?"

"I've got the numbers for all the sponsors of our guests."

"I want you to call Alice's sponsor. Find out if she's been in contact."

The night manager went around to his side of the desk and pulled out a drawer.

"Yeah?" came a voice through the telephone's receiver.

Delio pressed the handset to his ear. "Morry? It's Deal. One of the Hilton's residents has disappeared. I need your help."

"With what?"

"Finding her."

"Deal, my cell says it's ten-fifteen. She'll come home when the bars close."

"Morry, this is important."

"How important?"

"I've got the feeling life-and-death important."

"All right, how long's she been missing?"

"Three hours."

"That's it? Deal, we don't do anything until someone's been missing for twenty-four."

"Morry, she's A.A. You're A.A."

Silence.

Delio fiddled with the police detective's business card while he waited for Morry Gilman to say something.

The something came in the form of Gilman clearing his throat.

"Well?" Delio asked.

"Pick you up in ten."

A MAN STAGGERED out of the Company B Firehouse Bar, his coat misbuttoned and his cap screwed on half to the side. He plowed into Delio and Gilman coming up the snow-dusted walk. "S'cuse me," he mumbled. "Needa bum a ride. I'm too inebe, too inebe—too sloshed to drive."

Gilman flashed his badge.

The drunk stumbled back a step, and Gilman brought out his cell. He tapped open the jail's mug shot of Alice Ferrell and held it up to the drunk. "You see this woman tonight?"

"She in trouble?"

"No, she won the lottery. Have you seen her?"

"Not that I kin 'member. Need a ride. Kin I get one from one a yous?"

Gilman glanced up at a police cruiser coming his way. He waved it over and opened the back passenger door. "In," he said, aiming the drunk inside. "Watch it. Don't clonk your head."

He hooked the man into a seat belt and shoulder harness and, while he did, talked out of the corner of his mouth to the patrolman behind the wheel. "Take this guy home, Tommy, and, if he can't get in or hasn't got a home, take him to jail and let him sleep it off."

"Right, Detective. Want me to write him up?"

"Oh, come on, it's almost Christmas. Show a little love here."

"The night sergeant won't like it."

"You tell him for me tough tiddlywinks." Gilman closed the door. He slapped the roof twice, and the cruiser rolled away.

Delio clapped the detective on the shoulder. "Tough tiddlywinks?"

"What, you want I should say tough horse pucky?"

"Let him sleep it off? Don't ticket him? Gilly, you've got a heart of mush."

"Don't let the word get around."

They went on inside, a Christmas show running on the TV over the bar and nobody watching it. Delio looked up at the television. "That show, you know that one?"

Gilman glanced up. "Can't say as I do."

"It's a Jimmy Stewart special, *Mr. Krueger's Christmas*." He pointed. "See there, there's Stewart. He's playing Mister Krueger, a janitor, and right there in a dream sequence he's directing the Mormon Tabernacle Choir. This was filmed back in Nineteen Seventy-Nine."

"What, you're a television historian now?"

Delio hooked a thumb in his coat pocket. "Better. I was in it."

"The heck you say."

The bartender, built like a pro wrestler, sidled up. He slapped two Company B coasters on the bar, one in front of Delio, the other in front of Gilman. "What'll it be, fellas?"

Gilman flipped out his badge and brought his cell's screen up next to it. "This woman, has she been in here tonight?"

The bartender leaned down on his elbows. He studied the picture. "Alice. Yes, Alice Ferrell. No, 'fraid not. The last time she was in here was a couple weeks ago."

"What was she drinking?"

"Beer. That cheap stuff from Monroe. Said she was at the end of her disability check." The bartender scooped a pilsner glass out of the wash sink beneath the bar. He stripped the water off the glass and polished it dry with a towel. "Why you looking for her?"

"She's missing."

"Hmm." The bartender set the pilsner away with the other clean glasses on the back bar. From there, he reached up for the fire bell mounted next to the TV and ran the bell three times. A half-dozen heads turned toward him. "Anyone here know Alice Ferrell?"

One hand went up.

"You seen her anywhere tonight? I've got a cop here says she's missing."

The man shook his head and went back to his Jack and Coke.

The bartender planted his hands on the bar in front of Gilman. "Sorry. You want me to call around to some of our other places of refreshment?"

"We've been to all of them in the downtown. Yours is the last."

"Well, I'll still call around. Badges and police uniforms don't always inspire truthfulness among the people in my trade."

Gilman handed his business card across. "Call me if you find out anything."

DELIO AND GILMAN stepped back out into snow, the wind having come up. Gilman turned up his collar. "Look, I'll send an alert along with Alice's photo to the computer in ever police car we've got. That'll get us more eyes on the street, so maybe someone'll see her."

Delio hunched up in his mack, his hoodie pulled

down to his eyebrows. "You know, maybe the judge ought to order all us alkies and geek monsters to have one of those chip things embedded under the skin on our arm. That way we could ping someone who goes missing."

"That's a sci-fi world," Gilman said as the two stepped along toward The Homeless Hilton a block away. "So, tell me, if I can find *Mr. Krueger's Christmas* on Netflix, how will I know you? Which scenes are you in?"

"Only in one. I'm the skinny guy playing second trumpet in the Salvation Army band."

"You get Jimmy Stewart's autograph?"

Delio rummaged in an inside pocket for his wallet. He found it, brought it out, and, from an inside cavity, brought out a folded paper, the paper worn at the folds, the folds creases. This paper he passed to Gilman.

Gilman opened it. The cover page from a script, the title there—*Mr. Krueger's Christmas*—and the name of the screenwriter on the top half. Scrawled across the bottom half, *Young Mr. Delio, you sure swing on the brass. With respect, your newest best friend, James Stewart. Merry Christmas!*

Gilman refolded the page. "They're not gonna believe this down at the cop shop."

Delio clamped onto Gilman's arm. He hauled him to a stop. "No, this you don't tell to anybody."

"Why not? Deal, what are you hiding from?"

DELIO'S SUPERVISOR, sweat beading out on his forehead, grabbed him at the door to Santa Land. "Where's you line-'em-up elf? Where's Alice what's-her-name?"

"I don't know. She wasn't in her room when I left for work."

"And you weren't going to tell me?"

"Connie's going to cover for her, Bobby. She can do both jobs."

"Not well."

"Well enough. Really well if you give her her pay and Alice's pay, both."

The supervisor twisted away. He paced. "Deal, are you trying to rob me?"

"I'm just trying to get through to Christmas." Delio waggled two white-gloved fingers. "Two more days and we've got it done, man."

The supervisor scratched at the five o'clock shadow on the side of his face. "You really think Connie can do both?"

"Absolutely. We've got it worked out. Tell her she gets double pay for these last two days."

Delio fluffed up his stomach padding and went on out into Santa Land. As he took his seat on the throne, Elf Connie hustled in from the locker room, hustled up to him. "Bobby's gonna give me double pay for doin' my job and Alice's job. Did you have anything to do with this?"

"Ho, ho, no!"

DELIO RAPPED on the manager's door at the Homeless Hilton.

A woman's voice responded with "Come."

Delio opened the door, and the manager, Maria Razzota by the name plate on her desk, motioned him in. She leaned back in her chair. "Andy, how can I help you?"

"Maybe I can help you."

"How's that?"

He threw his leg over an armless side chair and sat down. "I've come into some money."

"Does that mean you're going to be leaving us?"

"And take on the hassle of renting an apartment, maybe having to find someone to share it with?" Delio gave a quick shake of his head. "No, I want to give you the money."

"For the Hilton?"

"And for the things this place does for people like me."

She leaned on her elbow on the arm of the chair as he brought out a wad of twenty-dollar bills, a thumb going under her chin and a forefinger up beside her face.

He counted out the money on the desk—seven hundred forty dollars. Delio pushed it to Razzota. "I want you to do two things with this. Divvy up two-thirds with the residents and take them on a shopping trip to the mall. Do it tomorrow."

"The day before Christmas? Andy, what a treat. And the rest?"

"On Christmas Day, take everybody out to dinner."

"Can I tell them who's buying?"

"No. Just say it's an anonymous donor. All the time you're getting anonymous donations."

"That's how we keep the doors open." Razzota held a bill up to her desk lamp. "This isn't funny money, is it?"

"It's real. All new bills I picked up this morning at the Fifth National. Call the bank president if you want. He'll confirm it."

"So how did you—"

"I'm Santa Claus. Well, at the mall, at least. But you can't tell anyone that, either."

"Of course. Nobody sees behind the beard." Razzota squared up the stack of bills. "Andy, you've been with us for almost a year. In all that time, I've never been able to figure you out."

"Isn't it nice to have a little mystery in your life?"

THE BIG BLUE People Shaker rolled up to the stop at the mall. Maria Razzota swung out of the first seat and raised her hand for the passengers' attention. "All right, everybody, you've got an hour to shop. At five o'clock, you meet me at Santa Land. We're going to take a group picture with Santa, then we're going to supper, all right?"

Scattered applause came from the passengers. They rose en masse and shuffled out into the aisle, working their way forward.

Razzota, now at the bottom of the steps, counted her charges as they passed by—thirty-seven with the last, Herbie Stein, a brain-injured vet hobbling down to the curb on two canes. "Herbie, you okay?" she asked after she checked him off.

"Fine, just not gonna win any races. As usual." He went on, trailing the others.

Razzota stepped back into The Shaker and waved up to the driver. "Babe, you'll pick us up at five-thirty?"

"Count on it, sweetheart."

"I can see why Andy Delio likes you so much."

"You know Deal? Ain't he sumpthin'? If I wasn't so well married, I'd get that fella for myself."

"AND I WANT a Play-All-Day Elmo, a Pie Face game, a Party Time Kitchen, a Girl Scout Cookies oven, a Shopkins Bubbleisha, an Exploding Kittens card game," the girl said, running off her list to Santa, Delio only half listening, wondering would she ever reach the end? Then he saw them, residents from The Homeless Hilton filtering into Santa Land, stopping in front of the lolly-pop fence, talking, laughing, showing off their purchases to one another, Razzota counting the residents against the list on her clipboard.

Herbie Stein slow-cruised up in one of the mall's motorized shopping carts, his canes and Christmas-wrapped packages in the basket.

The girl looked hard at Santa. "Are you listening to me?"

Delio blinked. "Exploding Kittens? Are you sure?"

"We're all playing it, but I don't have my own

cards for when my friends come to my house."

"I see. I'll make a note of that, dear." Santa stroked his beard. "But it seems to me that your list is awfully long. With all the other children in the world, you may not get everything. I hope you understand."

She jammed a fist into her waist. "I hope you understand my father's a lawyer."

He forced a smile and held up a candy cane.

She snatched it away, pushed off from his lap, and stalked off toward the picture-taking elf, Elf Connie.

Delio's supervisor materialized in front of Delio with Razzota beside him. He motioned back to the residents. "Santa, we have a group of people here who'd like to have their picture taken with you. It would be good publicity for the mall–homeless people given a shopping spree by an unknown benefactor. Whaddaya think?"

Delio gazed over the collection. He waggled a gloved hand at them, waggled for them to come forward, and the supervisor went about the business of arranging them around the throne.

Delio beckoned to Stein working his way up, the last of the Hilton's residents. "Want to sit on the arm of my throne next to me?"

Stein responded with a pained grin and continued up one step at a time. When he got up on the throne's platform, he turned and parked himself on the arm, pooching out his cheeks with a great exhale of breath.

Delio put a hand on Stein's leg. "You having a

good day, Herbie?"

An eyebrow jutted up. "How do you know my name?"

"I'm Santa Claus. I know everybody's name. Now tell me, what do you want for Christmas that you haven't already got for yourself?"

Stein, listing to the side, pushed against one of his canes and straightened himself. "I'd like to see my ma, but that's not possible."

"Where is she?"

"You don't know?"

"Herbie, I have so many details to keep sorted out, sometimes I get confused."

"Waltonville, Illinois. She's in the nursing home there."

"Waltonville. Let me see what my elves and I can do."

Stein rubbed his chin. "Boy, your voice is familiar. Do I know you?"

The supervisor clapped his hands. "All right, everybody, look right here," he said, moving over to Elf Connie. "We're going to take the picture."

She snapped three in rapid succession, studied them on the screen, made her selection, and waved an okay to the group. As they began to wander in bunches away from the throne, she tapped in thirty-eight and touched PRINT.

A patrolman, in a parka and boots, elbowed his way through and up to Santa Claus. He leaned down. "Santa. Mister Delio, Detective Gilman wants me to bring you to him. We've found someone."

DELIO, BACK IN his civilian garb, shoved the passenger door of the cruiser open and stepped out into dust devils of swirling snow. Ahead and down the slope from the street, closer to the river, flood lights illuminated a gathering of people—firemen Delio could see, a paramedic crew, a couple beat cops, and several divers in rubber suits with air tanks on their backs. Gilman, among them, knelt at the side of a rescue basket.

Delio ran down and stopped beside Gilman.

Gilman peered up at him. "Deal, I'm sorry, it's Alice. One of our guys walking the river trail spotted her body floating in an eddy below the dam."

He peeled a blanket back. "I'm thinking she jumped off a bridge upstream of the dam, probably Veterans Memorial. It's pretty high."

Delio's eyes clouded, and he twisted away. "But why? Why jump? Why now?"

Gilman laid the blanket back over the face. "God only knows, and He hasn't sent down any messages."

"But Christmas Eve?"

Gilman pushed himself up and swatted the snow from the knees of his trousers. "Deal, you're not going to do something stupid, like immerse yourself in a bottle of hooch, are you?"

"No." He looked up at the night sky, at the snow filtering down. "I think I'd like to go to church."

"All right, which one? I'll get you a ride."

"Saint Nicholas."

DELIO WAITED as the crowd from the early mass made their way out of the church and down the snow-covered steps to the streets, some talking, a few laughing, others silent, seemingly, by the expressions on their faces, at peace. When the last passed by, he made his way up and inside, into the warmth of the narthex, the air rich with incense and the scent of fresh pine greens.

He shoved his hoodie back and stripped off his gloves. At the holy water stoup, Delio dipped his fingers in and crossed himself, then went down the aisle. At the front, he knelt at the communion rail.

Behind him and above—from the choir loft—he heard some several people talking, women—a soprano and an alto—and another someone noodling on the organ, picking out a melody.

He felt a puff of air to his side as a door opened. Someone came in, stopped at the bank of vigil candles he figured from the silence, then came on. He felt a hand touch his shoulder.

"Deal, you're late for early mass and early for late mass. Are you all right?"

Delio crossed himself once more. He swivelled around and sat on the kneeling bench, leaned back against the railing.

The someone—a priest—sat down next to him. Father Roderigo Madrigal, called Father Rod by most. "So," Madrigal said, "what's going on here? Deal, you're not that good a Catholic."

"I'm a Methodist, you know that, trying to learn

your way 'cause it's so much more peaceful here."

"Come to bingo some Tuesday night. It's far from peaceful."

"Yeah, maybe. But here . . . and now." He drifted his hand through the air. "A friend killed herself."

Madrigal hugged his knees. "And on Christmas Eve when we celebrate a new life in the world that would change the world." He peered sidewards at Delio. "You're wondering what? Why?"

"Yeah."

"She one of the residents at The Hilton?"

"Yeah."

"Have problems?"

"Lots. Lots of demons in her life."

Madrigal let go of his knees. He stretched his legs out in front of him. "Maybe this was her way to peace. Yours was Hillybilly Heroin. Mine was Angel Dust."

"But you got your life right."

Madrigal placed his hand on Delio's knee. "You did, too, my friend."

"With your help."

"With Jesus' help and maybe a bit from me. How did your friend do it?"

"She jumped from a bridge."

Madrigal sucked on his teeth. "Have you thought that maybe Jesus was there and caught her soul before she hit the water?"

"Do you think?"

"I think I prefer to. See, my Jesus is a caring Jesus. So is yours."

"Still and all–"

"No still and all. You gonna stay for our next mass? It's Christmas Eve, Deal."

Rage
an AJ Garrison Crime Novel, book 2
"Terrifying. Just—terrifying. Timely and profound and even heartbreaking. Peterson's taut spare style and truly original voice create a high-tension page turner. I really loved this book."
– Hank Phillippi Ryan, Agatha, Anthony and Macavity winning author

The Last Good Man
a Wings Over the Mountains novel, Book 1
"Jerry Peterson joins the ranks of the writer's writer– that is, an author other authors can learn from, as in how to open and close a book, but also in how to run the course."
– Robert W. Walker, author of *Curse of the RMS Titanic*

Capitol Crime
a Wings Over the Mountains novel, Book 2
"In *Capitol Crime*, Peterson's vivid characters jump right off the page, and his sharp detail and snappy dialog puts the reader right in the middle of Prohibition-era action and one of the wildest schemes ever to take down a bootlegging ring. So buckle up. You're in for a hellava ride!"
– J. Michael Major, author of *One Man's Castle*.

Iced
a John Wads Crime Novella, book 1
"Jerry Peterson's new thriller is a thrill-a-minute ride down a slippery slope of suspense and shootouts.

Engaging characters, spiffy dialogue, and non-stop action make this one a real winner."
– Michael A. Black, author of *Sleeping Dragons*, a Mack Bolan Executioner novel

Rubbed Out
a John Wads Crime Novella, book 2
"Jerry Peterson's latest thriller gives us, once again, an endearing hero, a townfull of suspects, and quick action leading to a surprising climax. If you like your thrills to be delivered by strong characters in a setting that matters, this one's for you."
– Betsy Draine, co-author with Michael Hinden of *Murder in Lascaux* and *The Body in Bodega Bay*

A James Early Christmas and *The Santa Train*
Christmas short story collections
"These stories are charming, heart-warming, and well-written. It's rare today to see stories that unabashedly champion simple generosity and good will, but Jerry Peterson does both successfully, all the while keeping you entertained with his gentle humor. This should definitely go under your tree this season."
– Libby Hellmann, author of *Nice Girl Does Noir*, a collection of short stories

A James Early Christmas – Book 2
a Christmas short story collection
"What brings these Christmas tales to life is the compassion of their protagonist and their vivid sense of time and place. James Early's human warmth tempers the winter landscape of the Kansas plains in

the years after World War II. A fine collection."
– Michael Hinden, co-author with Betsy Draine of the Nora Barnes and Toby Sandler mysteries

The Cody & Me Chronicles
a Christmas short story collection and more
"Jerry Peterson is a fireside tale-spinner, warm and wistful, celebrating what is extraordinary in ordinary people with homespun grace."
– John Desjarlais, author of *Specter*

Flint Hills Stories
Stories I Like to Tell – Book 1
"Jerry Peterson's short stories are exactly how short stories should be: quick, but involving; pleasant, but tense; and full of engaging characters and engaging conflicts. I can think of few better ways to spend an afternoon than being submerged in James Early's Kansas."
– Sean Patrick Little, author of *The Bride Price*

Fireside Stories
Stories I Like to Tell – Book 3
"Witty and clever, Jerry Peterson spins a tale with a deft pen and an ear for dialogue that you don't find too often. There's an old-fashioned sense of character and craft in Peterson's works that will have you desperate for more."
– Sean Patrick Little, author of *The Bride Price*

ABOUT THE AUTHORS

Jerry Peterson writes crime novels and short stories set in Kansas, Tennessee, and Wisconsin.

Before becoming a writer, he taught speech, English, and theater in Wisconsin high schools, then worked in communications for farm organizations for a decade in Wisconsin, Michigan, Kansas, and Colorado.

Peterson followed that with a decade as a reporter, photographer, and editor for newspapers in Colorado, West Virginia, Virginia, and Tennessee.

Today, he lives and writes in his home state of Wisconsin, the land of dairy cows, craft beer, and really good books.

John Smith, a sophomore at the University of Iowa, is majoring in liberal arts. There, he's a member of the national championship improv troupe, Paperback Rhino. And he also does a Friday night stint—at midnight—on radio station KRUI 89.7 FM.

Smith writes short stories, poetry, plays, and film scripts. Inspired by Steve Martin, he also plays the banjo.

He comes from a family of performers and musicians. Smith's sister, Maggie, teaches at Chicago's Second City and performs there. And his sister, Sarah, is in NYU's film program. Both have been interns in the Hollywood film and television industries.

COMING SOON

Killing Ham, the third book in Jerry's John Wads Crime Novellas series.

36206715R00130

Made in the USA
Middletown, DE
27 October 2016